T0130132

Kingdoms
IN
Turmoil

BOOK TWO OF THE
DAWN HERALD SERIES

WARREN M MUELLER

BALBOA.
PRESS

A DIVISION OF HAY HOUSE

Balboa Press books may be ordered through booksellers or by contacting:

Balboa Press
A Division of Hay House
1663 Liberty Drive
Bloomington, IN 47403
www.balboapress.com
1 (877) 407-4847

Because of the dynamic nature of the Internet, any web addresses or links contained in this book may have changed since publication and may no longer be valid. The views expressed in this work are solely those of the author and do not necessarily reflect the views of the publisher, and the publisher hereby disclaims any responsibility for them.

The author of this book does not dispense medical advice or prescribe the use of any technique as a form of treatment for physical, emotional, or medical problems without the advice of a physician, either directly or indirectly. The intent of the author is only to offer information of a general nature to help you in your quest for emotional and spiritual well-being. In the event you use any of the information in this book for yourself, which is your constitutional right, the author and the publisher assume no responsibility for your actions.

Print information available on the last page.

ISBN: 978-1-5043-8598-5 (sc)
ISBN: 978-1-5043-8600-5 (hc)
ISBN: 978-1-5043-8599-2 (e)

Library of Congress Control Number: 2017912436

Balboa Press rev. date: 09/21/2017

CONTENTS

ACKNOWLEDGEMENTS

MY ACTIVE IMAGINATION, COUPLED WITH a fascination with fantasy and science fiction, have been formative in my interest of this type of book. It was my son, Jacob Mueller, who was instrumental in encouraging me to actually attempt to write a fantasy book. We both decided to begin writing such books together. It was this bonding that awakened a desire to take Biblical themes and weave them into a tale that merges human dreams with fantasy. I am grateful to my wife Diane and my nephew Carlton for their suggestions regarding the content of this book.

ANDHUN RETURNS

"ANDHUN! ANDHUN!" SHOUTED THE CROWD as he passed.

Andhun smiled and waved his arms in a sign of blessing as he rode in an open top carriage drawn by six white horses. The crowd pressed enthusiastically against two rows of soldiers who formed the walls of his route.

Andhun stood in the carriage with his staff in one hand. He seemed to dazzle the crowd. The sunlight reflected off of his white robe and pointed hat. His aide, Lagopus, sat at his feet basking in the adulation directed at his master. Few noticed his presence for the top of his head barely reached above the sides of the carriage. Those who did notice him thought he was a midget as his pointed ears were hidden beneath his curly black hair.

"Master, the whole world honors you as the greatest prophet of all time!" exclaimed Lagopus.

Andhun gave Lagopus a brief, condescending smile that turned to a frown as he replied, "Quite true for most but not yet for all. However, that shall soon change."

Lagopus nodded and said, "I have heard that King Thymallis refuses to convert despite the fact that most of his subjects including his son have done so."

Andhun replied, "The King is a stubborn old man who is set in his ways. We will soon confront him."

"What if he refuses to convert?"

"Don't worry. I have foreseen this day," replied Andhun with a smug smile.

Andhun rode at the head of a splendid parade of knights in armor, nobles and others of power and influence. They were an assembly of the most popular, wealthy and wise from throughout the kingdom. Like Andhun, they wore a medallion on their chest signifying their membership in the brotherhood of Andhun.

The procession moved slowly through the narrow streets of Eisendrath until they arrived at the Hall of the Kings. Lagopus opened the carriage door and stepped out before Andhun. He held a large copy of *The Once & Forever Ruler* above his head. As they ascended the steps to the Hall, the surrounding people dropped to one knee as a sign of respect.

One hundred trumpets announced their entrance into the great Hall which was filled with prominent people. Andhun noticed that less than half of them bore the medallion of their brotherhood. At the opposite end of the Hall, there were three thrones. Although he was too far away to see their faces, he judged that the King was seated in the center with his son and daughter on either side.

Behind them was a circular table with twelve thrones. The Kings of the earth had assembled here annually for the past one thousand years. With their next meeting approaching, Andhun decided to arrive before them and make this a decisive turning point in the history of mankind. As they proceeded across the hall with pomp and ceremony, some knelt while others stood in silence.

"Hail King Thymallis oldest and wisest among the Kings of earth!" exclaimed Andhun as he approached the first step below the thrones. The King sat sullenly and studied Andhun as he approached. He scowled as he stared at the book held by Lagopus. To his right sat his son Prince Olric, who bore the brotherhood medallion on his chest. He smiled fondly at Andhun as one admiring a legendary hero. His daughter, Princess Oriana, looked worried and tightly gripped the ends of her arm rests.

The King extended his hand whereupon Andhun advanced and kissed his signet ring.

"So this is the legendary Andhun!" said the King in an unimpressive tone. "I must confess that I expected someone younger and more vigorous. No doubt you probably think the same of me."

The King continued, "What is the purpose of your visit? It must be important to be conducted with such pomp and ceremony."

Andhun replied, "O great King, you have no doubt heard how the wisdom of this book before you has enlightened mankind. A new age of brotherhood and unity is sweeping across the kingdoms of this world."

The King interrupted, "Peace and prosperity we have had among the kingdoms for the past one thousand years. This has been achieved by a commitment to respect the differences among us. Peace has been maintained through compromise and finding common ground for the good of all."

Andhun tensed and his face became flushed as the King

spoke but then he seemed to catch himself and smiled as he said, "Well spoken! What you have said has worked well in the past but no more. The ways of which you speak were suited for a season in the history of mankind. We must learn to change and adapt to each new season."

The King responded, "Your words are eloquent and you have the appearance of wisdom. It is true that the number of converts to the ways you promote has greatly increased in recent time. Even my own son has converted. However, the brotherhood of which you speak appears to be only for those who join your beliefs. There is a spirit of pride among you and intolerance for those who do not share your beliefs."

Andhun's face darkened and he again became tense as the King spoke. "Do you oppose me?" he asked the King.

"With every fiber in my being!" replied the King. "You and your ideas have brought nothing but unrest and bloodshed among us. I will never renounce the ancient ways of my forefathers as described in *The Past & Future King!*"

At the mention of this book, Andhun became angry and sarcastically replied, "You are nothing more than a backward and ignorant old man! I have foreseen your lack of vision!"

Andhun stared defiantly at the King and said, "We shall pray for you."

He began to chant some words in an unknown tongue. His followers quickly joined him and soon the hall resonated with a thousand voices.

The King became angry and shouted, "Abomination!"

He rose from his throne and tried to speak but no words came out. A look of surprise and then fear appeared on his face as he gasped for air. The Prince and Princess leapt from their thrones and helped the King to sit down.

"Stop! You're killing him!" shouted Princess Oriana as she opened his collar.

Andhun and his followers continued to chant. The King turned blue and a gurgling sound came from his throat. After a few moments of struggling for air, he slumped onto the floor and died.

The apparent cause of his death was a heart attack. However, Andhun saw the wispy image of two bony hands appear around the throat of the King.

The Princess cradled her father's head in her lap and wept uncontrollably. So intense was her grief that those around her also wept. Even Andhun groaned inside and he experienced a brief moment of regret. He thought, "It is a shame that there was not some other way so that the death of this great King could have been avoided."

Andhun chastened himself for such thoughts, "Surely his death was necessary to accomplish the betterment of mankind."

He resumed his confident air and ascended the steps until he stood beside Prince Olric. He removed the crown from King Thymallis and held it over the head of the Prince saying, "The King is dead! Long live the King Olric!"

"Long live King Olric!" shouted a thousand enthusiastic voices.

The new King beamed gratefully at Andhun. Although he loved his father, he had waited many years to become King due to his father's long life. Except for his abrupt death, Olric could not have imagined a more honorable and glorious coronation.

"This is the greatest moment of my life!" he thought. "Andhun and the greatest of the brotherhood were gathered to proclaim me King! This is more than I expected in my wildest dreams!"

King Olric embraced Andhun. He took Andhun's hand and raised it above their heads saying, "My first proclamation as King is to declare that *The Once & Forever Ruler* shall henceforth be the official belief system throughout my kingdom!"

He turned towards Andhun and knelt on one knee as he said, "All that I am and all that I have I place in the service of the Brotherhood of Andhun!"

DISTURBING NEWS

"TAKE MY HANDS!" TOM SHOUTED to Willet and Cearl as their spirits flew over the Forbidden Mountains on a calm winter evening.

The clear sky sparkled with innumerable stars and Tom thought that this night was reminiscent of their first flight together at Taliesin. Tom's abilities had improved considerably during the past ten years. He had grown from a lad to a youth and was anxious to show off his improving skills.

Willet sighed and said, "Very well but I fear I will regret this."

He held out his hand and Cearl did the same so that Tom was between them.

Tom said, "Remember the first time we traveled like this in search of Lord Swefred's seeing stone? I believe you said that you carried me like a sack of buntatas. However, now I would like to show you something."

The trio accelerated to a speed that neither Willet nor Cearl had ever experienced before. They were moving so fast that the mountains below them passed in a blur. They looked at each other and laughed as their faces were distorted by the velocity of their flight. In a few moments, they crossed from Hadrian's Keep to the opposite end of the Forbidden Mountains near the Forest of Mordula.

Tom slowed them to a stop just inside the border. He looked at Cearl and said, "Well? What do you think?"

Cearl replied, "You have surpassed me. I felt like a sack of buntatas being towed."

"I believe your skills in astral projection rival those of the greatest of the elf lords and demonians," said Willet proudly. "It has been a wonder and a great pleasure to see how rapidly you have grown in many ways. Soon your training will be complete and…"

Willet suddenly stopped talking and closed his eyes. The furrows on his face grew deeper as he concentrated. Tom looked at Cearl and was about to ask him what was happening but he too closed his eyes. After a few moments, Tom heard a very faint but familiar sound that gradually grew louder.

"Look!" said Willet as he opened his eyes and pointed to the sky over the Forest of Mordula.

Tom saw a fiery red dot that rapidly increased in size until it split into six flaming demons who stopped abruptly about a mile away. A small yellow dot of light emerged from their midst and shot straight towards them.

"Cearl yelled excitedly, "Etain! It's Etain!"

Etain bowed and frantically reported, "I have been searching for you for many months. My lady, Princess Linette guessed that you may have sought refuge in these mountains but she refrained these many years from sending anyone to search for you. There are many spies among the elves and our loyalties have been divided since Lord Ceowulf's departure to Bane-ghial. However, Andhun's return to the world of men has forced her to risk sending me."

"Whoa! Slow down Etain! You say too much in too few words! I should like to hear a proper telling of these events in a more complete fashion," replied Willet as he stared intently into Etain's eyes. "However, I sense there is something else of a more immediate nature troubling you."

The small fairy looked down at her feet as if embarrassed.

Willet took her gently into his hands and said, "Come now little one, you are among friends. What troubles you?"

Etain replied, "I have risked much to find you. I fear I may have been too reckless in my determination not to miss the opportunity of this meeting."

She pointed to the demons in the distance and said, "There are many Pyrigians guarding the borders of these mountains. My lady commanded me to find you but not to be seen. She stressed the importance of not allowing the enemy to know what I know."

Tom interrupted, "You are safe with us! As you can see, there is some barrier that prevents the demons form entering these mountains."

Willet said, "I wish that it was that simple." He looked at Etain with concern and asked, "Where is your resting place?"

Etain whispered, "When I heard you conversing, I sensed that there might not be another opportunity as good as this one. I decided to risk crossing the border in spirit as it was the fastest way to reach you."

"Where is your resting place?" repeated Willet with growing concern.

Etain replied nervously, about five miles from here in the Forest of Mordula. I did not have much time to find the best resting place."

Cearl became alarmed and said, "The night is half gone and we must return to our bodies and retrieve Etain's before dawn!"

"Or before the enemy finds her," said Willet. "Look! The Pyrigians are dispersing! They go to find werewolves and others to search for Etain's body. If they can find it and possess her, they will discover much that needs to remain hidden."

Cearl said, "I fear they have a shorter distance to accomplish this than we do."

Willet smiled and replied, "That may be true but we have two advantages. One is that Etain knows the place."

"What is the other advantage?" asked Tom.

"You!" Willet replied as he held out his hand. "Show us how fast you can take us to Hadrian's Keep!"

THE RESTING PLACE

TOM'S MIND WAS SPINNING AS he rode Skreel towards the Forest of Mordula. He was filled with conflicting emotions resulting from the sudden rush of events that had changed his world. Part of him was excited by the prospect of new adventures outside of the confines of the Forbidden Mountains. At the same time, he was sad to be so quickly leaving the friendship of the dwarves and the Forbidden Mountains in which he had grown up. Willet said that Andhun's return to the world of men required that they too would soon have to go there.

Tom sensed that there must be grave danger before them as Willet had told them to put on the elvish armor from Dinwald's Deep. To wear this armor or even to touch it had been forbidden by Willet for the past ten years. He had instructed them that it was only to be used in times of great need. Despite his extensive training in military skills and tactics, Tom felt humbled and inadequate to be wearing such honorable apparel. Although he was nervous at the prospect of danger, there was an intangible presence that seemed to reassure him.

"Bear to the left!" Etain shouted to Willet as they rode the lead eagle. "Look! There is a disturbance in the forest ahead! That is where my resting place is! I fear that we may be too late!"

They soon arrived at the source of the commotion. In a clearing below, was a group of about thirty werewolves and several vampires. They had surrounded a single tree in a small clearing in the forest. Tom rubbed his eyes and blinked because he thought that the evening shadows must be playing tricks on him.

"The tree is fighting them?" Tom asked Skreel.

Skreel replied, "It must be some magic at work! Hold on! We are going in!"

As if by some unseen signal, all of the eagles dived in unison into the midst of the werewolves.

In the chaos that ensued, Tom found himself hovering near the base of the strange tree. As Tom and Skreel fought the surrounding werewolves, Tom's senses and fighting skills seemed to be enhanced as though he were being helped by some unseen presence. A sudden burst of light from Tom's stone temporarily blinded some of the nearby werewolves. In the glow of the seeing stone, Tom discovered a large demon near the tree. He was reaching towards Etain's lifeless form as if to take possession of her body. Tom felt a strange surge of energy and he sensed that he had to keep the demon from touching her so he said, "Do not touch her foul fiend!"

The demon turned towards him and laughed cruelly as he said, "You are no match for me young fool! I shall possess my prize and then torment you!"

A voice within Tom replied, "I am no mere youth! Behold! I am Sir Egric of the Aigneis!"

The spirit of a mighty elf lord emerged from within Tom and attacked the demon.

Skreel shouted to Tom, "Hold on! I'm going to get Etain!"

Skreel swooped to the base of the tree and grabbed Etain's body. Tom placed her body inside his chest armor. They began to escape when Tom noticed a vampire flying after them.

"Vampire in pursuit!" Tom told Skreel who gave a loud screech and began to accelerate.

Despite the speed of their flight and several evasive maneuvers, the vampire closed the distance between them. Tom could see that this vampire had body armor and appeared to be of noble rank. He remembered that Willet had told him vampires could only be killed by piercing their heart or by cutting off their head.

He signaled Skreel, "Barrel roll when he gets close!"

Skreel gave a scream of acknowledgement.

When the vampire was about to overtake them, Tom shouted, "Now!"

Skreel looped back over the on-rushing vampire and rolled as the vampire passed beneath them.

Tom released his grip on Skreel and drew his sword. He landed on the shoulders of the vampire and plunged the blade through the neck and into his heart. Tom and the deceased vampire dropped like two stones until Skreel dove and caught Tom.

Skreel looked down at the battle below and said, "The werewolves have been slain or have fled!"

Tom said, "Let's find Willet and Etain!"

"No need," replied Skreel. "I see her spirit approaching."

Tom held Etain's lifeless body in his hands for a few seconds until it suddenly came alive as if from a deep sleep.

Etain said, "We must make haste to return to the clearing!"

An Unexpected Parting

"WELL DONE MASTER TOM! VAMPIRE slayer! You have become a formidable foe!" said Willet with a grin. "Well fought one and all!" continued Willet as he slapped Wini on the back and then gave Min a slight bow. "You have learned much and, though there is always more to learn, I am proud as a father who has seen his children well grown."

Willet motioned for Tom and the others to come to him.

"Gather around! We don't have much time!"

Willet stood beside the lone tree in the center of the clearing. Scattered about were the bodies of slain werewolves. Tom was relieved to see that all but a few dwarves and one eagle had survived the fight.

Tom noticed that Willet suddenly looked sad and tears welled up in his eyes as he said, "Dearest friends, the time of our parting is at hand." He turned towards King Raegenheri and said, "May the Creator bless you for your kindness and hospitality. In all of my long years, I have never known a more noble king. It has been an honor and a privilege to know you and I shall ever be in your debt."

Willet bowed towards the dwarves and then embraced the King. He then turned towards Min and said, "Farewell gentle giant! Your humility and willingness to serve have been an inspiration to us all! Despite our physical differences, you have become a son to me. Where I go you cannot follow. I have left instructions for you in a sealed envelope at Hadiran's Keep. I shall treasure you in my heart until we meet again!"

Min wept as he hugged Willet and lifted him off of the ground.

Willet continued, "Etain, please return to Princess Linette and inform her of our plans."

Etain bowed and said, "I shall tell her all you have said and conveyed to me telepathically." Their eyes locked for a brief moment as they exchanged thoughts. The sound of horns in the distance broke their concentration.

King Raegenheri said, "The sentinels sound warnings that the enemy returns. We shall meet them to give you more time to escape. The King commanded, "Sound the attack!"

Several dwarves blew their horns in reply and the eagles bore them towards the warning sounds.

Willet said, "There is one more thing to do before we depart." He walked to the tree and said, "Hail, noble spirit! Remember and speak!"

The tree began to quiver and a low murmuring sound was heard deep within it like someone clearing their throat. A face appeared in the trunk.

"Who are you?" asked Willet.

"My name is Tondbert," replied the tree. "I was once

a dwarf. It has been many years since gnomes cast a spell on me."

"I know this magic," replied Willet. "Unfortunately, it has been too long since your transformation to reverse the spell."

Willet continued, "We are forever grateful for your help in defending Etain."

"It was my honor and privilege," replied Tondbert with a bow.

Willet said, "It is a pity that we do not have time to further make your acquaintance. We must make haste to leave but, before we do, I have a gift for you in gratitude for your service."

Willet paused and concentrated as if recollecting something deep in his memory. His face relaxed and he smiled with satisfaction as he said, "Meamna a goll er ash! Aillens a coisich!"

Tondbert began to shake starting from his top down to his roots. Tom and the others stepped back in amazement as Tondbert's roots erupted from the ground and he started to move about on them like they were feet!

Willet said, "You now have the gift of mobility and speech. If there are others like yourself, you may impart these gifts to them by repeating the words that I have just told you."

Tondbert smiled and said, "Thank you very much! From now on I shall be called Tondbert Tree Walker. I shall search for others and help them as you have helped me! I am forever in your debt. You have loosed my bonds from the earth! I feel new energy and purpose in life!"

Willet smiled and said, "Farewell Tondbert Tree Walker!

You had better leave this place as we now must do with as much speed as possible."

They quickly mounted their eagles and followed Willet in the opposite direction from that taken by King Raegenheri. As they left that place with great speed, Tom looked back and could see the top of Tondbert's branches moving quickly through the Forest of Mordula.

"Where are we going?" Tom asked Skreel.

"To the nearest portal," was the reply.

On the horizon ahead there was a faint, flickering glow that Tom recognized as a portal. In the east, the sky was getting lighter and soon it would be dawn.

As if in response to these thoughts Skreel said, "Hold on! We fly like the wind!"

The last of the human spirits disappeared into the portal as they approached. The glow in the eastern sky told Tom that it was a matter of minutes before the first rays of the sun signaled the closure of the portal. Skreel breathed heavily and Tom sensed that he was straining from the sustained maximum effort to arrive before the sun. The portal was a small pond in the Forest of Mordula. Willet was just ahead and Wini was close behind.

Skreel said, "It's going to be close! Jump into the portal as soon as we are over it!"

Tom was about to ask why they didn't just dive in together when Skreel shouted, "Now! Let go!"

As if to make sure that Tom didn't hesitate, Skreel suddenly rotated. This surprised Tom and caused him to drop like a stone into the portal. Tom braced for the impact but, instead of hitting water, he found himself falling into a glowing tunnel. Willet dove off of his eagle at the same instant and was just ahead of him. Looking backwards Tom felt his stomach tighten and he felt dismayed to see nothing but the empty sky above the surface of the pond.

"Wini! Wini!" shouted Tom but there was no reply.

The first rays of the sun reflected off the pond just as Wini hit the surface with a splash. Within seconds, Penda grabbed him and pulled him out of the water.

"Don't worry Master Wini. I've got you!" said Penda. "We shall try again tonight. Now we must make for Hadrian's Keep!"

THE BLACK HORSE INN

$\mathscr{A}$MHAS AND TWO OTHER TROLLS sat at a large wooden table near the hearth of The Black Horse Inn. The hour was late and many of the patrons had turned in for the night. They had been drinking heavily for most of the night and were competing at telling tales of their adventures. One of the trolls, named Kork, was telling a story about a giant, one-eyed Cyclops who lived in a cave deep in the earth.

"I'm telling ya it was full of treasure!" swore Kork as he took a deep drink from his tankard.

"Bah! I don't lieve it!" stammered Amhas. "If he was sleep'n, why didn't ya steal some of the treasure?"

Kork drained the rest of the ale and slammed his tankard on the table. He wiped his mouth with the back of his hand, leaned over the table towards Amhas and said, "Cuz of the bones!"

"Wha d'ya mean?" said Amhas as he squinted and tried to focus on Kork's face.

"The bones! The place was ful o them! Twas all sorts of things that it had eaten!" replied Kork.

Amhas sneered and said, "So ya have no proof! Hard to lieve without proof!" He looked at the other troll and said, "I thought we were tell'n real stories not child's tales!" They both started to laugh which irritated Kork.

Kork's face and ears flushed deeper red and he clentched his fists as he said, "I suppose ya never had anything happen t'ya tha was hard to lieve without proof!"

"Well in fact I have something even harder to lieve!" said Amhas with an air of wounded pride.

"Alright then, spit it out!" shouted Kork. "It's gett'n late and I could use a bed time story!"

Kork slapped the other troll on his back and they both started to laugh.

Amhas felt a sudden rush of blood to his face as he replied, "How bout a traitor troll with a seein stone who kills his own kind to save elves and men!"

Kork and the other troll were shocked by this and there was momentary silence as they tried to visualize this statement. They looked at each other and then burst into laughter.

"Tis true I tell ya! We wuz bout to trap some elves and a boy with a seein stone when this troll ambushes us and leaves me for dead! They fled to a secret place called Hadrian's Keep!"

Kork snorted, "Never heard of it! There's no such place! Seein stones are very rare and only elf lords hav'em! Tis convenient that they disappeared to a place that doesn't xist!"

At the mention of the seeing stones, a short hooded

figure emerged from a table in the shadows nearby and said, "Hadrian's Keep does exist! I have been there!"

The three trolls turned towards the hooded figure and froze at this unexpected apparition.

"Who are you?" asked Amhas.

The cloaked figure removed his hood and said, "I am Miran, Chief among the gnomes and prophet of *The Once & Forever Ruler!*"

The trolls stared in shock and amazement at this legendary figure.

Turning towards Amhas he said, "I shall go to Hadrian's Keep and test the truth of your words!"

The room became momentarily dark as a sudden rush of wind caused the fire in the hearth to flicker. The wind coincided with the swift flight of Gorbash up the chimney and into the night sky.

"Molech will be pleased to hear of these seeing stones, the missing lad and the strange troll," he thought to himself as he flew to the nearest portal.

A second spirit also left the Inn after hearing this news. However, this spirit left in a cautious and secretive manner. Edric hid in the rafters of the Inn as was his custom. This Inn was the place that Prince Ceowulf had assigned to him. For the past ten years, he had faithfully kept this nocturnal vigil without hearing anything of importance.

He could feel his pulse racing as he thought about the significance of this news. "This will set a new course for thousands of his brethren and end ten years of futile searching for the seeing stone destined for Lord Ceowulf."

THE HALL OF THE KINGS

*L*AGOPUS STOOD ON A STOOL and assisted Andhun with his robes. He then placed the miter on his head as they prepared for the annual meeting of the kings.

"Today is a historic milestone in the development of mankind," Andhun beamed as he finished dressing.

"Yes Master! It is very exciting and somewhat unreal to think that all our hopes and dreams are about to finally happen!"

Andhun replied, "I hope that all of the kings will accept and enforce the ways of *The Once & Forever Ruler*. However, even if this happens, there will be some who will resist."

"Then they shall be crushed by the power of the united kingdoms!" exclaimed Lagopus.

Lagopus lowered his voice and whispered, "We could even further enhance our power and advance our cause if you would bring some creatures from the first earth."

Andhun scowled at Lagopus and said, "Do not speak of this again! I have told you that I will decide when the time is right! Everything must be done in the proper order! Your impatience reveals a lack of faith and wisdom."

Lagopus knelt at Andhun's feet and grabbed the hem of his long robe. "Forgive me Master! I only wish to see you succeed to your honor and the glory of Devlin!"

Andhun mechanically extended his hand and Lagopus kissed the ring he wore with the emblem of his order. He barely heard the apology as he was troubled by other thoughts.

"How did I do it?" he pondered.

Andhun began to review thoughts that he had wrestled with many times since Lagopus had emerged with him into this second earth age of mankind. Such a feat had never been done before and he felt quite proud of his accomplishment. However, he did not know exactly how he had done it. Previously, the only creatures of flesh to pass between the earths were humans and this was only done from the second to the first age. Through years of study and careful preparation, he and members of his order had discovered how to travel back from the first to the second earth. However, no other creatures of flesh had ever passed between the two earths. He had traveled back to the first earth several times and tried to bring his saber tooth tigers and other creatures to the world of men but he had failed. His pride kept him from admitting his failures to Lagopus.

"It is better that his faith and devotion are not shaken," he thought to himself. "Besides, I am sure that I will discover the secret soon."

King Olric stormed into the room and slammed the door behind him.

"She is stubborn and narrow-minded, just like her father!" he complained to Andhun. His mood suddenly changed and he looked worried as he said, "Yet, she is my sister and I love her. I fear for her safety if she continues to oppose us."

Andhun placed his arm around the King's shoulders and said, "Your feelings serve you well. We can not allow her to become a rival for our opponents to rally around. If she will not convert, perhaps arrangements can be made through which she will still serve our purposes."

King Olric looked alarmed and asked, "What do you mean?"

Andhun stroked his beard and seemed to think aloud, "I have heard that some of the kings are wavering in their allegiance to our new order. King Vulpes is the most influential among them. Hasn't he previously expressed interest in your sister?"

"She would rather die than marry him!" replied King Olric.

"For the sake of your sister, let's hope that is not necessary. Come! It is time for us to greet your royal guests," said Andhun as he grabbed his staff and led them to the throne room.

King Vulpes was the last to arrive. After being announced, he proceeded to the front of the great hall and ascended the stairs to the platform holding the table and twelve thrones. He walked over to his customary place and stood between the table and the throne embossed with the head of a serpent.

Andhun stood at the head of the table which was traditionally left vacant. This place was held in highest honor. The kings would take turns addressing the council from this position. Before him on the table was a large copy of *The Once & Forever Ruler*.

Andhun sized up each of the kings as they filed into the hall and took their places. He noted that six kings including Olric wore the medallion of Andhun's Order. King Vulpes and two others seated next to him did not. Andhun strove to look composed and confident while inside he became anxious and then angry at the absence of three kings. Never in the past one thousand years had all of the kings, or at least their delegation, failed to appear for the annual council.

"Welcome most noble kings of the earth! Today marks a new beginning in the history of mankind. The old ways set forth in *The Past & Future King* have been replaced by new revelations of truth and wisdom described in *The Once & Forever Ruler*. Rejoice and be glad for this new order promises to bring about an improvement and perfecting of the unity, peace and prosperity of mankind!"

Six kings shouted an enthusiastic, "Amen! Make it so!"

King Vulpes asked, "What's in it for us? How will this new order benefit us?"

Andhun smiled and said, "The wealth and power of those who oppose us shall be given to the faithful. By their absence, three kingdoms have spurned the traditions of this council and the privileges of the new order. Therefore, their titles, rights and possessions shall be forfeit unless they repent and whole heartedly embrace our cause."

Andhun paused and looked at King Vulpes, "As for you Lord Vulpes, I believe something special that you have long desired could be arranged in exchange for your undying allegiance."

Andhun waved his hand in the direction of Princess Oriana as if presenting her to King Vulpes. The King's face immediately brightened at the prospect of this possibility.

Princess Oriana was seated nearby among the other nobles and dignitaries. She immediately rose and shouted, "I am not a play thing or possession to be bartered!"

She stormed from the room and slammed the door behind her.

After a brief but awkward silence, Andhun smiled and said, "She has a strong spirit and it will take someone up for a challenge to make her a suitable wife."

King Vulpes responded, "I am up for the challenge!"

"Then step forward and embrace *The Once & Forever Ruler!*"

King Vulpes rose and nodded to the other two kings next to him. They also rose and followed his lead. Lagopus appeared from behind Andhun and picked up the copy of *The Once & Forever Ruler* from the table. The three kings knelt before Lagopus and Andhun. Each swore allegiance to uphold the ways of *The Once & Forever Ruler.* Andhun produced a gold chain necklace and medallion for each king from a pocket in his robes. After kissing Andhun's ring and their medallions, they arose in unison.

The great hall resounded with cheers as the other kings rose and joined Andhun and the three new converts. They faced their subjects and joined hands raising them above their heads in a sign of solidarity. The cheers of the crowd increased and they began to shout, "Praise to Andhun! Praise to Devlin!"

After basking in the adulation of the crowd for several minutes, Andhun motioned for silence and said, "Now brothers please sit down and let's begin to plan the conversion or destruction of those who have yet to join our cause."

An Awkward Meeting

Tom looked back at Cearl who began to fade and then disappeared as they approached the other end of the portal. Willet grabbed Tom's hand and shouted, "Close your eyes!"

There was a brilliant flash of light that temporarily blinded Tom despite having closed his eyes. When he regained his sight, he was standing on a large flat rock beside a slow moving stream. A few steps away there was a beautiful young woman lying on her stomach while sun bathing with her eyes closed. Tom was embarrassed and intrigued by the sight of her as she was naked.

Before she could react, Willet covered her mouth with his hand and said, "Don't make a sound! We will not harm you!"

He removed his cloak and covered her. Then he looked deeply into her eyes and asked, "Are we in danger?"

The young woman nodded yes and then motioned for him to be quiet.

Willet removed his hand from her mouth and she whispered, "Shhh! Be quiet or you will be killed!"

Willet asked, "Who are you?"

She whispered, "I am Princess Oriana of Eisendrath."

"Where are your clothes?" asked Willet.

"They have taken them so that I do not run away. I am betrothed against my will to King Vulpes. I am being escorted to his kingdom where we shall be married. Can you help me escape?"

"Where are your captors?" asked Willet.

"In the surrounding trees are my hand maidens. They are forbidden to look upon me until I give permission at which time they will approach behind a blanket. I shall wrap myself in it and accompany them to the camp which is a short distance into the woods."

"Can you swim?" Willet asked.

The Princess nodded yes.

"Then follow us," said Willet as he motioned for Tom to get quietly into the water.

They swam to the opposite shore and then floated downstream under the cover of brush and grasses that hung over the steep riverbank. After they had floated for several hundred feet, Willet motioned for them to gather beside a larger boulder.

"Stay here! I shall be right back!"

Willet disappeared under the water while Tom and the Princess waited nervously for his return. Tom was both happy and terrified to be left alone with the Princess. His heart pounded and he tried hard to appear calm but every time he looked at her he found it hard to breathe.

After the longest minute of Tom's life, Willet emerged and said, "Follow me!"

The river was about ten feet deep near the boulder. Willet dove straight to the bottom and entered a small hole in the bank near the rock. Although the water was clear, Tom could not see anything as he pulled himself through the submerged tunnel. He began to worry about how long he could hold his breath when he emerged into a small air pocket above an underground stream.

"That's the worst of it!" said Willet "Watch your head!"

They swam or rather bobbed in the current of the underground stream. In some places, the water almost reached the roof of the cave. After bumping his head several times on stalactites and projecting rocks, they arrived in a much larger cave.

Willet said, "Remain here while I find a light."

After shuffling around in the dark and stubbing his toe, Willet found some flint and produced a torch. Tom was surprised to see that this was no ordinary cave. There were rugs on the floor and walls, wooden furniture and plenty of books. On the far side of the room there was a tunnel that Tom guessed must be the preferred entry way. There was even a notch in the wall that looked like a fireplace.

"Welcome to my home or rather what was once my home before I moved to Downs End," said Willet wistfully as if remembering the details of his younger years.

"First we must put on some dry clothes."

Willet walked over to an old trunk and opened it. Inside were various sizes of clothing. While Oriana rummaged through the trunk for something to wear, Willet took Tom aside and whispered, "This place was once an active portal to the home of Princess Linette in Taliesin. However, it became unstable and is no longer active. I spent many of my younger years here and am quite familiar with the surrounding country."

"These are all boys clothes and some are quite well used," Oriana complained as she held them up for size.

"They are such as I was growing up," commented Willet. He selected some loose fitting articles for her and said, "Forgive me, my lady but it will be necessary for you to disguise yourself as a young lad. We shall call you Olaf. I regret that your hair must be cut short."

"I will gladly become Olaf to avoid becoming the bride of King Vulpes!" replied Oriana as she put on the clothes in a dark corner of the cave.

After proper introductions, Willet baked some cakes made from grain stored in a large wicker basket. While they ate, Oriana explained the events that led to their encounter. Willet looked worried when she mentioned the rapid progress that Andhun had made in uniting nine of the twelve kingdoms. His worry turned to sadness and then anger as Oriana related how those who refused to convert were imprisoned or even killed for holding to the old ways in *The Past & Future King*.

Oriana suddenly changed the subject by asking, "How did you appear so suddenly and silently beside me?"

Tom and Willet looked at each other and were momentarily at a loss for words. Then Willet replied, "I am a magician and Tom is my apprentice."

Oriana sensed that there was more that they were not telling her but she played along.

"Wonderful! I have long wondered how magicians appear and disappear! Perhaps you could teach me?"

She seemed to enjoy the brief exchange of uneasy looks between Willet and Tom. Willet cleared his throat and said, "Of course, my lady. We shall teach you some errrrr tricks in due time if you remain with us."

Willet continued, "We must remain here for awhile until your suitor and his companions cease to look for you in this area. Meanwhile, make yourselves comfortable. There are plenty of good books to read."

When it was time to sleep, Oriana laid down on Willet's bed while they laid on some rugs at the opposite side of the room. When Willet was sure Oriana was asleep, he whispered to Tom, "It is time to fulfill my oath. Tonight we go to see your father."

THROM'S VISION

$\mathcal{G}$ORBASH AND SEVERAL OTHER PYRIGIANS accompanied Throm's spirit to the nearest portal much as they had done for the past ten years. They had faithfully carried out Molech's orders to keep a constant watch over Throm. At times, Gorbash would wonder at the wisdom of continuing their vigil as nothing unusual had happened. He was glad that they rotated their watch over Throm so that he was sometimes freed from this boring duty. They joined a swelling river of human spirits and entered a portal while Gorbash was preoccupied by other thoughts.

The first indication that things were going to be different tonight happened quickly as they emerged in a fountain of spirits in the first age of the earth.

"Convergence!" shouted Gorbash as they found themselves in the midst of a swarm of competing spirits. There were more elves than he had ever seen. Before they could react, they were engulfed by a wave of elf spirits. While Gorbash battled several elves, he noticed that a wizard and a young man appeared and flew away with Throm.

"Father! It's me, Tom!" he shouted as they flew back through the portal.

"Tom? Is that you?" His father's spirit seemed groggy like their previous encounter many years ago. His father looked at him and said, "You don't look like Tom, and yet, there is something familiar about you."

"Where are we going?" Tom asked Willet.

"To your house," was his reply. "It is the last place that the Pyrigians will look first."

When they arrived at the farm, the sight of his sleeping parents filled Tom with sadness as he observed how they had aged since he had seen them last.

Once Throm's spirit returned, Willet spoke into his father's ear.

"Throm, wake up! Tom and Willet are here to see you!"

"Eh? What?" mumbled Throm as he rolled over. "Just another dream." However, he opened one eye and what he saw caused him to bolt upright into a sitting position in bed. His jaw dropped open and he rubbed his eyes as if to clear his vision.

Standing or rather hovering about a foot off of the floor at the foot of his bed were two shining ghostly figures. One he recognized as the old scribe Willet. However, the other was a teenage youth dressed in a strange suit of armor. There was a brightly glowing stone around his neck.

The youth said, "Father! It's me, Tom!" He approached as if to hug him.

"Stay away from me! Leave me alone!" Throm shouted.

The spirit of Tom's mother suddenly appeared and

re-entered her body. Tom gave Willet a worried look but Willet said, "It's alright Tom, the elves have temporarily occupied her escorts."

His mother awoke and hugged Throm saying, "Hush, my dear. It's just another one of your bad dreams."

"No! They're right there! Look!" Throm replied as he pointed towards the foot of the bed.

"She can not see us Throm," said Willet.

"Why not?" asked Throm.

"Because she doesn't believe in spirits," replied Willet.

"Stop it! You're scaring me!" screamed his wife. She sat between them on the bed facing Throm. She grabbed his face and said, "Look at me! You have to get hold of yourself and reject these wild delusions!"

Willet started to chant something and suddenly Tom's spirit began to regress in age until he was the young boy that Throm remembered. Throm pretended to look at his wife's face but he actually was mesmerized by the vision behind her. As Willet continued to chant, Tom's spirit accelerated in age until he appeared as before.

Willet stopped chanting and told Throm, "As you have seen, there is no doubt that this is your son."

Tears began to well up in Throm's eyes and he said, "Tom! It is you! You have returned!"

His wife screamed, "Throm! Darling! Please! You're loosing your mind!"

Willet said, "We are as real as you. Search your heart! Remember what you have learned as a boy! Return to the lake and find your destiny!"

Throm's face slowly brightened as if he remembered

something that had long been suppressed or forgotten. He smiled strangely and whispered, "Yes, I'm coming!"

His wife shook him and slapped him as if to shock him back to reality saying, "Throm! Snap out of it!"

Throm pushed her gently aside and said, "The lake! I remember! I'm coming!"

Willet said to Throm, "You must hurry! Others may return at any time and confuse your mind."

Tom's mother shouted, "Stop! Throm don't leave me!"

Throm replied, "I have to go." He turned and started running towards the lake.

His wife yelled, "I'm getting help!" She ran to the next farm house.

As Tom and Willet accompanied Throm, Tom noticed that it was a calm summer night similar to the one he experienced long ago. When they arrived at the lake, Throm climbed onto a large boulder beside the shore. As he stared at his reflection, Tom's image replaced his and said, "When you see the vortex, you must jump into it and then we shall be together again!" Tom's image faded as the water began to stir. Throm hesitated as he watched the calm surface transform into a swirling vortex.

"Stop!" screamed his wife as she ran towards him with her neighbor.

As they approached, Throm looked back and forth as he decided what to do. She stretched out her hands towards him and spoke in a soothing voice, "Darling, everything is going to be fine. Just come with me and I will help you forget about the nasty spirits that trouble you."

Throm's face changed as though he discovered something and said, "You don't understand. I see now that your persuasive helpfulness has blinded me. All these years, I have denied what my heart has told me was true because I trusted your judgment."

Throm looked back at the swirling vortex. A pleasant but unknown voice beckoned him to, "Take a leap of faith if you would know the truth!"

His wife tensed and said, "Throm! Look at me! Keep your feet on the ground!"

Throm looked at her with fear at these words but his fear quickly passed. He smiled at her as he said, "I love you Heidi!" He then turned and jumped into the vortex.

"No!" Heidi fell to her knees and sobbed uncontrollably as Throm disappeared into the vortex. Tom was overcome with grief as he felt the gravity of her loss. He wanted to comfort her and give her hope. As his stone started to glow, he stood beside her and placed his hands over one of her ears and shouted, "Do not fear! Have faith! It is not the end but the beginning!"

She stopped crying and whispered, "Tom! Is that you?"

As Throm sank into the vortex, Willet told Tom, "We must return at once. The hour is late and the enemy will soon return."

"Please, I wish to go with my father!" Tom pleaded.

"Do not worry. You will see him soon. He will be well tended."

"How do you know that?" asked Tom as he recalled his passage through this portal.

"Cearl is waiting for him," replied Willet as they returned the way they had come.

Oriana stooped over Willet and Tom. She waved her hands back and forth before their eyes but there was no response. She feared that they were dead but, when she placed her hand over Willet's mouth, she felt a faint passage of air. She bent over Tom and was about to place her head on his chest when he abruptly awoke. She blushed and withdrew her hand from his chest. After an awkward moment of silence, she regained her composure and asked, "What were you doing?"

She looked at them suspiciously and said, "I have never seen anyone sleep like that before!"

Willet and Tom exchanged worried looks and then Willet tried to calmly say, "My lady is very perceptive! What you observed is a special kind of meditation that we magicians do."

"Fascinating!" replied Oriana with a shrewd smile. "It seems to me that there is more to your magic than some cheap carnival tricks. I should like to know more of this magic!"

THE SCROLL

King Rhaengheri summoned Wini and Min as soon as they returned to Hadrian's Keep.

"The King looks very old and tired," Wini thought to himself as they approached his throne. He sensed that the recent battle and change in their fellowship had drained the King.

They bowed and stood silently before his throne waiting for him to acknowledge them. The King seemed deep in thought as he sat on his throne and stared at the scroll on his lap.

After several minutes, his gaze shifted to them and he said, "Dear friends, it appears that recent events have altered the course of our lives. I fear that perilous times lie before us that will test our faith and friendships."

He unrolled the scroll to reveal another sealed one inside it. He extended it towards Wini and said, "Please take this."

Wini bowed and took it from the King who said, "Several months ago, Willet gave me this scroll and asked that I keep it sealed until after he departed from the Forbidden Mountains. He told me that he had a vision which he was not permitted to share except for what has been written in this scroll. The outer scroll was addressed to me and I have just read it. However, he did not speak of another scroll hidden within. This scroll bears your name Wini."

Wini's hands trembled as he broke the seal and read:

Dear Wini,

When you read this, we shall have parted ways. I want you to know that over the past ten years I have grown to love you as a son. I know how your concern for Tom and I must be causing you great distress so I have written this to console and counsel you.

It is imperative that you do not attempt to follow us. Your path lies with your people. You must make haste to return in spirit to your homeland and warn your King that his life is in danger. He is one of three kings that remain true to the ways of "The Past & Future King" and so has been targeted by assassins.

I have every confidence that you will obey my wishes and that you have the skills and wisdom to accomplish this task.

Farewell until we meet again.

Willet

P.S. Please hand this scroll to Min. I have written a few words for him on the back of this scroll.

Wini looked up to see Min and King Rhaengheri standing together and staring at him in expectation. The contrast in age and size was great but the look on their faces was so similar that Wini smiled as he said, "You both have the look of a new father who is about to be told whether he has a boy or girl."

After a brief laugh, Wini said, "My heart is heavy for I must soon leave this place for my home land on urgent business. Before I take my leave, there are additional instructions for you Min."

Wini handed the scroll to Min but he just looked at it. Min fell to his knees and pleaded, "Please read it for me Master Wini. I feel as though I am loosing my friends one by one until I will again be alone. I can not bear the thought of being sent somewhere alone!"

Wini turned the scroll over and read:

To Min, most excellent troll and true friend,

Do not fear. Your path does not yet require you to forsake these mountains. Nevertheless, you must forge new friendships while retaining ours.

You must go to those of your race who come to these mountains and bear witness to the truths you have learned.

I am confident that you will find new friends if you remain true to us and the ways of "The Past & Future King."

With great expectation for your success, I look forward to our next meeting.

Your friend,
Willet

STRANGE APPARITION

SHYLAH WARMED HIMSELF BESIDE THE fire, he was tired from searching the mountain slopes and discouraged by the continued false reports of an entrance below the surface of the Forbidden Mountains. For the past two weeks, they had searched several mountain valleys that ended in sheer rock walls. Occasionally, they found rock clefts, overhangs and even a few caves but none of them went anywhere. There were about forty trolls in his party including many seasoned warriors. They were heavily armed and well provisioned for a long search. The werewolves that accompanied them constantly scouted their perimeter for any signs of ambush. Nevertheless, he was on edge and sensed that they were being watched He took comfort in the presence of Ultan and Cragmar who sat beside him.

Ultan spat into the fire and said, "I say these mountains are either empty or there are too few dwarves to find!"

"Perhaps we are chasing ghosts," Cragmar mused.

"Bah! Them be wives tales!" snorted Ultan.

Cragmar replied, "If that's true, then why have none who have entered these accursed mountains returned?"

Ultan spat again and said, "Stupid orcs and fool trolls seeking Devlin's pleasure have gone before us not mountain trolls and seasoned warriors such as us. Look around and you can easily see why these are called the Forbidden Mountains. Sudden mountain blizzards, avalanches and treacherous terrain explain their disappearance."

"Don't forget about the gnomes!" said Shylah.

"Exactly!" shouted Ultan as he slapped him on the back. "There's got to be many times more gnomes than dwarves in these mountains based on the arrows and other weapons we found with the dead orcs we found yesterday. Now stop fretting and get some sleep."

Several hours after Shylah fell asleep, he was startled by a brilliant green light. He shielded his eyes with his hands and waited for his eyes to adjust to the light. When he ventured a peak between his fingers, what he saw caused him to think that he must still be dreaming. He rubbed his eyes to clear his vision and to assure himself that he wasn't dreaming. In their midst, stood the transparent image of a troll unlike any he had ever seen. He was dressed in glistening armor that was embossed with figures and inscriptions that bore witness to his nobility and power. At his side there was a large, two-edged broadsword with a jewel encrusted hilt. Around his neck he wore a glowing stone on a silver chain that pulsated with energy that bathed him in a halo of green light. Shylah was frozen in reverent fear in the presence of such a magnificent and imposing apparition while the trolls around him were thrown into an uproar of confusion.

"I am Min, light bearer, son of the dawn and guide to those chosen to know the truth!"

Ultan jumped to his feet and shouted, "Lightening storm! Take cover in the rocks!" He tripped over Shylah as he grabbed his things and hurried to the nearest group of rocks.

The wind suddenly increased in intensity and it started to rain but Shylah continued to be mesmerized by the awesome vision.

Min said, "You shall know true friendship, joy and peace if you join me. Tomorrow night I shall return to gather the elect."

The vision faded and Shylah scrambled to find shelter with Ultan and the others.

"I've never seen so much lightning! I told ya that these be inhospitable places!" Ultan shouted towards Shylah and Cragmar.

"Aye! This certainly is a brawny storm! But what say ye about the voice? I tell ye twas a ghost that was speaking!" whispered Cragmar as he shivered.

Ultan spat and sneered, "Bah! Your ghost superstitions about these mountains are playing tricks with your mind!"

Ultan slapped Shylah on the back and said, "Tell him mate! There was nothing more than thunder playing games with his imagination!"

Shylah looked down at his hands and remained silent.

"Come on! Speak up! Tell this squeamish excuse of a troll that there was nothing unnatural about this storm but its intensity."

Shylah looked up at them and said, "I not only heard a voice but I saw it too!"

Ultan's smirk melted away and his jaw dropped in

disbelief. Cragmar shuddered and pulled his blanket tighter and over his head.

The next night, Shylah could not sleep. He had lost respect with Ultan who clearly thought he had lost his nerve or his mind. He could have recanted but the vision was so powerful that he could not think of anything else. Consequently, he had become the object of ridicule, taunting and bad jokes.

"What if the vision of Min doesn't happen again?" he asked himself. Even if nothing happened, he had discovered that those he admired and trusted had turned on him. He decided that the real illusion was the loyalty and trust he had placed in them.

It was nearly dawn when Min reappeared. This time he said nothing but merely beckoned for Shylah to follow him. As he quietly rose to follow Min, he noticed that Ultan and the other trolls slept deeply. He carefully stepped over and around his sleeping comrades and was surprised to see two other trolls also following Min. They converged near the edge of the camp where Min turned and whispered, "Say nothing, no matter what you see or hear! Do not look back or return!"

Shylah fell in line behind the other trolls. As they continued to leave the camp behind, Skylah wondered what happened to the sentinels. As if in answer, he saw the forms of two werewolves emerge from the darkness. At first, he thought they must be sleeping but, when they passed by, he could see they had been killed by numerous arrows.

Min led them up the side of a mountain overlooking the camp until a horn blast signaled the attack. The ground around them seemed to erupt as hundreds of dwarves appeared from hidden places before and beside them.

Min turned and said, "Stay close to me and do not look back!"

He then continued to walk up the slope as though nothing unusual was happening.

Below them, Shylah heard the sounds of confusion and alarm as the dwarves converged on their camp. He felt torn between the urge to turn and help his comrades and his desire to know more about this vision. Suddenly, one of the trolls ahead of him turned and yelled, "Ambush! Death to the dwarves!" He ran about ten steps back towards the camp before he fell dead from a dozen arrows.

Min stopped and again turned towards them. His face was filled with sadness at the sight of the fallen troll. He looked at them and pleaded, "You must trust me! Stay close to me and within the glow of the stone! It is not far now!"

Shylah saw something that he had never seen before in any troll. "Compassion! Min somehow values us and feels responsible for us!" he mused.

The sounds of the battle quickly faded to silence. Shylah surmised that the end came quickly for everyone in the camp. Faced with certain death below and adventure above, Shylah decided to keep climbing.

Assassins

*W*INI'S SPIRIT PASSED THROUGH SEVERAL walls, halls and corridors as he followed the beam of light from his stone. He soon arrived at two massive wooden doors with ornate engravings. Two guards stood on either side of the doors but they did not notice anything unusual as Wini walked between them and through the doors. Once inside the King's bedchamber, the beam of light rested on the face of a gray bearded man that Wini surmised must be the King of Redwald.

"Arise Sire, for you are in grave danger!" said Wini as he bent over the King and spoke into the his ear.

The King sprang from the bed producing a dagger from beneath his pillow. There was a burst of brilliant light from Wini's stone that caused the King to drop his dagger and cover his eyes with his arms.

"Who are you?" whispered the King.

"I am Wini, light bearer, son of the dawn and guide to those chosen to know the truth!"

"Truth? The world has been divided by it. Do you hold to the old or new truth?"

"There is only one truth as you know in your heart, O King. I hold to the ways of *The Past and Future King* as you do," replied Wini. "My time is limited and my message is urgent. Assassins have been sent to kill you. They will be here before dawn. I shall return as soon as possible. Farewell!"

As the image of Wini faded, the King shouted, "Guards!"

Immediately, the guards rushed into the room to find the King alone.

The King muttered, "Either the strain of these troubled times has affected my mind or I have seen a vision. In either case, be vigilant in your watch as I fear there may be assassins about."

Several hours after dismissing the guards, the click of the door handle turning on the glass doors leading to his private veranda woke the King from troubled dreams. He continued to lie still as though sleeping while he slowly moved his hand under the pillow. As he withdrew the dagger, he lurched from his bed and shouted, "Guards!"

There was a brilliant flash of light that temporarily blinded everyone in the room. When the King recovered, he found himself fighting someone completely covered in black except for his eyes. His opponent was much quicker and was well versed in the martial arts. He was soon bleeding from wounds to his shoulder and side that would have been worse if he hadn't barely managed to deflect the blows at the last instant with his dagger. He was surprised and encouraged to see Wini join his guards in fighting several other assassins

The fight was fierce but brief as the assassins were lightly armed with daggers and relied on stealth. Wini quickly dispatched one of them and then eliminated the King's opponent from behind. The other two assassins fled out the glass doors to the veranda after killing one of the guards as they entered the room.

"How did you know?" asked the King.

"I saw them while traveling here to warn you. I also saw that the armies of King Abban and Bruddai have crossed the border. They are loyal to Andhun and are marching here to replace you with someone loyal to their cause. They will be here in three days."

"Treacherous dogs! I never trusted either of them!" said the king as he held his side and winced in pain. "We shall march to meet them in two days."

Wini replied, "You are outnumbered and wounded, my Lord."

The King grimaced and said, "Then we shall even the odds."

Wini tore the sheets and wiped the blood from the wound on his shoulder.

The King winced and said, "As for my wounds, they shall find how dangerous this old badger can be when wounded and cornered!"

The King paused and looked curiously at the open glass doors to the veranda. "I wish to know more about you and your strange comings and goings. Tell me, how did you arrive right behind the assassins?"

"I am a magician of sorts," replied Wini.

"Aye, so ye must be. That and much more it appears from the look of that strange armor."

THE PLAINS OF REDWALD

"THIS PLACE STINKS OF SHEEP!" complained King Abban as he led his army across the Plains of Redwald.

"Aye! There's nothing to see but grasslands and sheep in two days of marching," added King Bruddai. "This is no proper kingdom. I don't see why Andhun thinks two armies are needed to conquer such a desolate place. Based on what I've seen, less than half of one army would be enough."

King Abban laughed and said, "Take solace in the fact that the end is near. I'll wager that by this time tomorrow, there will be a new King of Redwald!"

"Aye! The only resistance seems to be these accursed sheep! Out of the way! Yaah!" yelled King Bruddai as he spurred his mount to quicken their pace.

The two armies marched in ranks of six men wide to prevent becoming too strung out as they traveled. They continued to be amazed and annoyed at the vast number of sheep that grazed around them. It was mid-day when they reached the crest of one of the many rolling hills in the broad grassland. As they reached the crest, they stopped abruptly for in the road before them stood two men clothed in sheep skins. One was old and hunched over as he leaned on a wooden staff. The other was much younger with black curly hair and beard.

The younger man raised his hand and shouted, "Halt! In the name of King Torin of Redwald, stand and state your business!"

King Bruddai flushed red with anger and replied, "Insolent peasants and stinking sheep! Kneel and crawl of out the way or I'll have your heads on my lance!"

The old peasant removed his sheep skins to reveal his armor and said, "The King of Redwald kneels to no man!"

Before they could react, King Torin raised a ram's horn to his lips and blew it. The sheep that were placidly grazing around them suddenly stopped and then converged on the foreign armies.

Mayhem ensued as thousands of sheep hemmed in the armies and began to bite the horses and foot soldiers. A second horn blast announced the appearance of thousands of soldiers as the army of Redwald emerged from trenches and trap doors covered with turf. The soldiers of Redwald formed two lines behind the sheep on both sides of the road. They carried slings, bows and javelins. They targeted the opposing bowmen first and then the horsemen. The invaders found themselves hemmed in by strangely aggressive sheep and engulfed in withering volleys of arrows, javelins and sling shots.

King Bruddai spurred his horse and lowered his lance towards King Torin. Wini pushed King Torin aside and dodged the end of the lance. He grabbed the shaft and buried the point in the ground which caused King Bruddai to vault over the head of his horse. Before Wini could finish him, King Abban drew his sword and attempted to decapitate him. Wini dove under his horse and cut the saddle strap. As he emerged on the other side of the horse, King Abban leaned towards him and lunged at him with his sword. His saddle came loose and King Abban fell at Wini's feet. Wini finished him with a dagger to the throat before he could recover.

Wini looked about and saw King Bruddai exchanging sword blows with King Torin. Although King Torin fought bravely, he was being driven backwards as he was weakened from his wounds. Wini realized that he would not survive much longer without help. Before he could reach him, Wini was knocked over from behind by a wave of sheep. He struggled to stand but could not regain his feet due to the jostling masses of sheep. As he crawled about seeking some space to stand, he encountered a pair of human legs. He looked up to see King Torin looking down at him.

The king laughed and said, "Though your dress and ways are strange, you are no doubt of Redwald blood for the sheep treat you as one of their own!" King Torin extended his hand to Wini and his face became grim as he said, "Let's finish this business. Many of our dear sheep have sacrificed themselves to spare the lives of our kinsmen. I am determined to end this bloodshed as soon as possible."

The king blew his ram's horn and the soldiers of Redwald converged upon the remnants of the two invading armies which were quickly subdued before they could organize a counter attack. Wini fought beside King Torin who refused to rest despite his wounds.

When the fighting ended, the King leaned upon his sword

and said, "The proud and powerful brothers of Andhun shall be stunned by today's victory and hope shall be renewed."

"Quite true," said Wini. "However, our enemies will return in greater numbers and they will not be so easily surprised."

The king thought about this in silence and then replied, "Then we shall not wait for their return. Let's strike while we have surprise and momentum on our side. Word has reached me that Andhun and the armies of five kings march to Lochlemond. It is there that the fate of the kingdoms will be decided."

Wini smiled and said, "So be it. Let's hasten to meet our destiny."

MIRAN'S RETURN

*M*IRAN AND HIS GRANDSON CEBU emerged from the narrow ravine and left the stream bed to cross the hidden valley before Hadrian's Keep. Miran walked slowly with one hand on Cebu's shoulder and the other on a wooden staff that bore a white flag. He paused frequently to catch his breath and to wipe the perspiration from his face.

"Cebu, my child, remember what I have told you. My end is near but your destiny lies before you."

Cebu's face filled with worry and he pleaded, "Please don't speak like that! Devlin has protected you and has granted you a long life. He will not fail us in our time of need."

Miran looked down at his grandson with pride and said, "I am encouraged by your faith. However, from this moment on we must no longer speak kindly of Devlin. No matter what happens, you must hold Devlin and his truths in your heart while embracing the ways of the dwarves with your lips."

Cebu asked, "Is there no other way?"

Miran stopped and looked sternly into Cebu's eyes. "You must never doubt or deny what I have told you! Devlin has given me a vision in which our brethren will return and conquer these mountains. In order to accomplish this, we must gain the trust of the dwarves."

Before he could continue, a voice shouted, "Stand and identify yourselves!"

While they had been talking, a group of dwarves suddenly appeared out of a nearby creek bed.

"I am Miran, chief of the gnomes and this is my grandson, Cebu. We are pilgrims seeking to see the sacred stone in Hadrian's Keep."

The leader of the dwarves stepped forward until his face was close to Miran's and said, "I am Dehlin, son of Behlin. If you are who you claim to be, you are the last person I would take to the sacred stone for your perverted ideas have poisoned and divided our race."

Miran assumed a feeble and humble manner and replied, "It is as you have said. It has taken most of the years of my life living in exile to come to the realization that I have been wrong. I have returned to beg forgiveness and to renounce the ways of Devlin."

Dehlin was dumbfounded by this confession and paused to consider what to say. Before he could respond, Miran's eyes suddenly got very large and a surprised look appeared on his face. A trickle of blood came from his mouth and then he fell forward revealing three orc arrows in his back.

Garash, who was the captain of the orcs, crawled forward through the tall grasses with several of his best archers until they were in range of Miran and the dwarves.

"Kill only the old one on my signal," he whispered to the

archers. "He is too slow to run and may cause the others to fight rather than flee."

Garash signaled the archers and they loosed a tight volley of arrows that traveled horizontally several feet off of the ground until they struck the old gnome simultaneously in the back. Once Miran fell, Garash and the archers stood and charged the group of dwarves growling and yelling as they advanced. Their cries were immediately drowned by those of several hundred orcs that emerged from the cover of the same ravine that Miran and Cebu and recently traveled.

Dehlin rolled Miran over and saw that he was dead. He then grabbed Cebu and ordered the dwarves to retreat towards Hadrian's Keep. While they were running, he took a burlap sack out of his pocket and put it over Cebu's head. Cebu struggled to return to his grandfather until Dehlin knocked him out with a blow from his hand.

Garash and his raiders were pirates who had been promised a king's ransom in gold if they followed Miran and discovered a hidden passage into the Forbidden Mountains. For several weeks, they had shadowed the ship that carried Miran until it reached the mouth of the river. It was easy to follow the old gnome but they had been fortunate to surprise several dwarf sentries before they could raise an alarm.

As they ran across the valley floor in pursuit of the dwarves, Garash congratulated himself that everything was going according to his plans. He had the foresight to instruct his followers to not outrun him. He wanted only to be close enough to see where the dwarves would disappear through some hidden door and then they would retreat and report their findings.

The fleeing dwarves ran directly towards a sheer rock

wall at the opposite end of the valley. At the last moment, a door appeared and they disappeared just as Garash had expected. He noted the place but pretended to lead his raiders slightly off to one side as if confused about where they had gone. When he reached the rock wall, a horn blast sent a shiver down his spine. Garash stared in horror as many doors appeared in the rocks around them and thousands of dwarves poured out of them.

Garash shouted, "Retreat! Back to the ravine!"

He turned and ran back the way they had just come only now they were the prey instead of the predators. He noted with dismay that dwarves were descending from the mountains on all sides of the valley. He decided that their only chance was to reach the ravine where they could neutralize the greater number of dwarves in its narrows. A desperate foot race ensued in which he adjusted his direction several times to avoid pursing groups of dwarves. His lungs began to burn and his legs felt like lead weights when the approached the entrance to the ravine. Despite his exhaustion, his spirits soared and he raised a battle cheer at the unexpected appearance of twenty trolls. The trolls emerged from the ravine and rushed straight towards them.

Garash yelled, "Hail, brother trolls! Most welcome..." He stopped speaking as he sensed something was wrong. These trolls were dressed strangely in armor that looked elvish!

In a matter of seconds, the on-rushing trolls met them and fear gripped him as the trolls raised their clubs and swords. The last thing Garash saw was a troll, with a glowing green stone around his neck, raise his club and deliver a crushing blow to his head.

Hidden in a fir forest high above the valley floor, Lord

Ceowulf and a handful of elves watched the demise of Garash and his raiders.

"Look there my Lord!" said Edric as he pointed towards the group of trolls converging on the fleeing orcs, "Is not the leader of the trolls wearing a glowing seeing stone?"

"Yes! That's the renegade troll who has my seeing stone!" replied Lord Ceowulf.

Edric looked puzzled and several moments of silence passed before he asked, "Why are the trolls attacking the orcs?"

Now it was Lord Ceowulf who thought for several moments before replying, "I don't know but I'm certain there's treachery of some sort going on. The dwarves are a half breed race that has long ago withdrawn from the fellowship of elves and men. I am not surprised that a rogue band of trolls has found refuge with dwarves!"

Edric said, "According to legends, these mountains are called Forbidden because there is some force that protects the dwarves."

"Bah! Superstitious nonsense! Did you not see how the dwarves appeared from the rocks? It is not some mysterious force but rather a form of rock lore that I'll wager we can learn and use to our advantage." Seeing that Edric continued to look troubled about the action below, Lord Ceowulf slapped him on the back and said, "Come! We shall learn this rock lore and return to see what lies within these mountains!"

REFLECTIONS

TOM THOUGHT ABOUT HOW MUCH his life had changed in the past two weeks. He missed Wini, Min and many others at Hadrian's Keep who had become his family over the past ten years. He thought about the Keep, Dinwald's Deep and other places in the Forbidden Mountains that he regarded as his second home. Even as he longed for a visit, even just in spirit, he recalled that Willet had forbidden him to return in any manner since the mountains were closely watched by the Pyrigians.

On the other hand, there was always hope that circumstances would require a visit to the Forbidden Mountains. After all, Willet had forbidden him to visit his parents and they had recently made a surprise trip. He smiled and his heart burned with joy as he remembered his father's passage into the first earth age. He and Willet had visited Throm in spirit several times since his arrival in the Valley of Glainne where he dwelt with Cearl and Prince Caelin. Each night since the first night that Oriana had joined them, they had taken her spirit with them to Glainne, Taliesin and many other blessed places. Willet said it was best to bring her along so that she would not again find them in a trance like state when they traveled in spirit. Besides, Willet said she would sleep better than normal but would remember little of the elves and the blessed lands that they visited.

Willet had decided that it was time to leave the cave in which they had been hiding. He led Oriana and Tom on a narrow path that Tom surmised must be a deer trail. As Tom walked behind Oriana, he stared at her as if in a trance. Despite the loose fitting clothing which hid her figure, he detected a feminine stride that could only be noticed upon close inspection. Tom thought of her beauty. He noted her slender build and short-cropped, golden hair beneath her deer skin hat. He pictured her fair face with fine features and deep blue eyes.

How wonderful and frightening were the thoughts and emotions that ran through his mind since he met her. It seemed like she filled every moment of his days. He thrilled to make her laugh and chastised himself when she did not approve of his attempts to impress or amuse her. His heart pounded and his throat constricted at the touch of her hand. He thought about asking Willet if what he was feeling was normal but did not because he was afraid to share such powerful and personal emotions.

Oriana sensed that Tom was looking at her but she continued to walk ahead of him without turning around. She enjoyed the attention and was more often than not amused by his attempts to impress her. While she was flattered that he found her attractive, she did not want their relationship to progress beyond friendship. Although he was handsome, he was not of royal blood and so could not be considered further. Besides, he was darker, taller and leaner than the type of man she had pictured as her future husband. Nevertheless, there was something mysterious and intriguing about both Tom and Willet. She enjoyed riddles, challenges and novelties. These two appeared ordinary but she sensed that there was something extraordinary about them.

"Magicians indeed!" she mused to herself. She had been entertained by many magicians and prided herself on her ability to detect or figure out the methods behind their "magic." She was sure that she would find the reasons for their strange sleeping behavior. In the meantime, she found them to be kind and good people and she enjoyed their company. Besides, she was grateful to them for rescuing her from an abominable marriage.

She was puzzled by how they had appeared so suddenly beside her while she was sun bathing. "I must have dozed off," she thought. However, she could have sworn that she had just closed her eyes and then opened them. Her father and others had told her that she had a keen sense of hearing. From a young age, she was able to not only identify forest animals but could tell their direction and distance.

"I hope my senses are not growing dull," she thought as she focused on various sounds in the forest. Having reassured herself, she returned to thinking about her present circumstances. Andhun had poisoned her brother's mind and she was determined to rescue him and restore their kingdom to the ways of their father. She did not yet have a plan that seemed feasible but she felt that she was on the right path.

They had waited in the cave for over a week before Willet said it was safe to leave. King Vulpes searched for her day and night until he was forced to leave by promises made to Andhun. During their stay in the cave, Oriana recounted the events of her father's death and the meeting held by Andhun in the Hall of the Kings. She was surprised but pleased that Willet decided to take her to King Alric, who was her uncle and one of the three kings who rejected Andhun and his beliefs. However, she was beginning to wonder if Willet knew where he was going. Since leaving the cave, they had avoided any roads. Based on the sun, they changed directions many times each day. Occasionally, they would pause and Willet would withdraw a short distance from them. Sometimes she could hear him mumbling as though he were talking to himself or someone else.

For the most part, Willet was amused by the youthful teasing and enjoyed the laughter that Oriana brought to their company. She was a spirited young woman of strong convictions who was not afraid to speak her mind. The furrows in his forehead grew deeper and then a slight smile appeared on his face as he thought of her.

"She's intelligent, curious and beautiful but as unpredictable as the wind."

He had thought the best course was to proceed to the Kingdom of Lochlemond which was the strongest of the three kingdoms that opposed Andhun. However, Oriana had persuaded him to change his mind once he learned of Andhun's plans. At the council of the kings, she learned that Andhun planned to eliminate King Torin of Redwald and King Alric of Strathyre first and then send the full might of his armies against the kingdom of Lochlemond. To accomplish this, Andhun commanded that Redwald and Strathyre be invaded by the nearest four kingdoms loyal to him. Kings Abban and Bruddai were sent to Redwald while Kings Ronan and Whon invaded Strathyre.

During their last night in the cave, Etain brought news of Wini and the defeat of Kings Abban and Bruddai. Therefore, Willet knew that Wini and King Torin were marching to Lochlemond. While encouraged by this news, he knew that it would take the united efforts of all three kingdoms plus some luck and careful planning to have a chance of defeating Andhun's combined armies. Thus, it was critical that King Alric be persuaded to march to Lochlemond as soon as possible. Willet knew that this would not be easy since King Alric was indecisive by nature. In addition, he was surrounded by advisors that were under the influence of the Pyrigians. This made it impossible to warn him in spirit.

He continued to walk in deep thought as he reflected about their unexpected encounter with Oriana. While he knew the place where the portal would deliver them, he wondered at their awkward yet fortuitous meeting. During his many long years, he recalled various events where the needs of many were met by the convergence of seemingly unrelated circumstances.

Who could have foreseen that they would arrive at precisely the right time to rescue Oriana from an unwilling marriage? She was the niece of King Alric who had banished Willet from his kingdom many years ago after refusing to listen to his council. Thus, Willet knew that he needed Oriana to persuade her uncle to march to Lochlemond. Even with her help, the outcome was far from certain due to the influence of the Pyrigians over his trusted advisors.

Willet knew that the Creator worked in mysterious and unexpected ways. He sensed the Creator's purpose but not his plans in the decision to change their destination from Lochlemond to Strathyre.

Was there anything significant in the youthful bantering between Tom and Oriana? What hidden needs did they have that might be met from such a chance encounter? While he pondered these and many other things, he did not sense that they were being watched.

CYRIC OF CAMLIN

ORIANA AND TOM WERE COMPETING in a game of who could best identify forest animals by their sounds when a heart stopping scream came from the forest just ahead of them. Willet's face became white and he tensed as he lowered his staff in the direction of the sound. Oriana and Tom cautiously approached and stood beside Willet. Tom looked at Willet who stared intently at the underbrush before them. He tried to appear brave but he feared what sort of beast could make such a horrific sound. As he slowly withdrew his sword and prepared to face the beast, he glanced at Oriana to gauge her reaction. Much to his surprise, she looked quite calm and was smiling at him. He looked at Willet who suddenly relaxed and started to laugh. Tom realized the he had been tricked by Oriana. He smiled with embarrassment as he looked at the drawn sword in his hand.

"You both looked like you had seen a ghost!" laughed Oriana.

Tom replied, "You sure fooled me with that sound. I have never heard anything like that before!"

"Nor have I in this world," muttered Willet. "Where did you learn that sound?"

Oriana flushed and said, "I didn't learn it. I made it up." She looked away with embarrassment and said, "I wanted to frighten you so I chose a sound that has frightened me."

She raised her eyes to meet Tom's and he saw fear in her soul as she said, "It is the sound of a beast that has haunted my dreams!"

There was an uneasy silence during which Tom noticed that Willet seemed to be struggling with what to say. Finally, Willet looked at Oriana and said, "I see that you have the ability to imitate and project sounds. Can you also do voices?"

Oriana smiled and Tom was surprised to hear his voice shout from the underbrush before them, "Help! The beast has me!"

"Impressive!" exclaimed Willet. "However, such talents should not be trifled with."

"I'm sorry!" replied Oriana. For a moment she looked down and appeared to be humble and repentant. When she looked up at Tom, her mood abruptly changed. She smiled mischievously and said, "Though I regret my methods, you must admit that I frightened you!"

They shared a nervous laugh and then resumed their journey.

Several hours later, they reached a stream with clear and cold flowing water that had been partially held back by a landslide from the base of a mountain on the opposite side. After replenishing their drinking water, Willet led them across the boulder strewn dam. As they stepped from one rock to the next, Tom succumbed to an urge and pushed Oriana from behind. She fell into the pool on the upstream side of the riffle and was completely immersed.

At first, Tom and Willet laughed but then quickly stopped when Oriana remained underwater. Tom crouched down on the boulder that Oriana had stood on and peered into the water. He saw a shadow rising rapidly from the depths. Suddenly, two hands emerged from the water and pulled him in. The shock of the cold water caused him to take in water so that he emerged coughing and gasping for breath. As he splashed about and struggled to orient himself, he felt Oriana grab him around the neck and pull him to the boulder. His embarrassment at being so taken off guard and then rescued was matched by a sudden rush of joy. When she turned him around, he looked into her eyes and saw concern for him on her face.

"Are you OK?"

Tom nodded his head yes and continued to cough up water.

Willet said, "I believe his ego has been damaged more than anything! You two are a sorry sight! Why I've seen drenched cats look and fare better than you two!"

As Willet laughed, Tom caught a look from Oriana and they both suddenly grabbed Willet's robe and pulled him in.

They laughed and splashed water at each other until they reached the far bank where they climbed onto a large flat rock. As they lay on the rock and enjoyed the warmth of the mid-day sun, Tom felt a slight vibration and opened his eyes. Willet and Oriana were already on their feet sensing the source of the disturbance. Tom was about to ask what was happening when the vibration became the low rumbling sound of approaching horses. Before they could react, thirty horsemen emerged from the nearby forest and surrounded them. They wore full body armor and each carried a long lance which they leveled at the surrounded trio as they hemmed them in.

Their armor was unknown to Tom but Oriana's face blanched and she said, "They are knight's of King Vulpes!"

They were forced together until they stood back to back facing a circle of lances. For a few tense moments, they stood silently until one of the knights raised his visor and said,

"What have we here? Willet is that you? You look like a drowned rat!"

Willet replied, "It takes one to know one!" Then he addressed Tom and Oriana, "These men are not knights but scoundrels and thieves!"

The knight who spoke looked offended but quickly regained his composure and introduced himself.

"I'm Cyric of Camlin and these men are far nobler than those whose armor they wear!"

"How did you come by such distinguished apparel?" Willet asked.

"We dropped in on some of the King's men for breakfast the day before last. They were less vigilant than normal so it was easy to overpower the few sleepy guards and surprise the rest. We woke them up with the end of our swords. It seems they had spent the previous week searching day and night for a princess that had disappeared and so were quite exhausted. We took pity on them and sent them on their way in their noble underwear!"

After a hearty laugh with his men, Cyric suddenly became serious. He looked at Tom and Oriana and then said to Willet, "What manner of folk dare swim with the likes of Willet? Please introduce us to your companions."

Willet replied, "These are Tom and Olaf who are pupils of mine."

"Olaf indeed! The clothes and haircut are those of a young lad but the form is definitely female!"

Willet and Tom looked at Oriana and noticed that her loose fitting clothing was clinging to her figure. Oriana was suddenly aware that everyone was staring at her. She looked down at herself and tried to pull her shirt away from her body but it kept clinging to her so she finally crossed her arms in front of her. While she was thus preoccupied, Cyric withdrew a blanket from a saddle bag and handed it to her.

"Given recent events, your disguise and royal figure, may I call you princess?"

Oriana grabbed the blanket and wrapped herself in it.

Before Willet could reply, Oriana assumed a regal pose and said, "You will address me as Princess Oriana of Eisendrath!"

Willet rolled his eyes and was about to protest when Cyric beamed, "With pleasure your highness!" and he bowed and offered her his hand. "You honor us with your presence. We shall provide a much more suitable escort for one of such high and noble birth!" With a wave of his hand, the lancers backed off and he escorted her to his horse.

As Tom watched Oriana and Cyric walk away, he felt a burning sensation in the pit of his stomach. He was suspicious of this fancy and fraudulent knight. He was also concerned about how easily Oriana had warmed to his flattery. He was about to challenge Cyric, when he felt Willet grab his arm to restrain him.

"Let them be!" Willet whispered in his ear. "We must bide our time and not offend our new host!"

Reluctantly, Tom followed Willet's example and climbed behind one of Cyric's knights while Cyric took the mount of one of his men.

Turning towards Oriana, Cyric said, "It shall be my honor to provide you with fine dress more suited to your highness. If my lady can forebear those rags until the end of the day, I shall be able to transform you into a proper princess."

Oriana smiled at him and replied, "I should greatly appreciate a hot bath and bed again."

Cyric said, "You shall have both and I shall personally make sure that they are to your liking." As soon as his men formed two ranks of riders behind him and Oriana, he spurred his mount and shouted, "To Camlin straight away and without further delay!"

Mayhem

*T*HE RIDE TO THE NEAREST road was mercifully short for Tom. Hard as he tried, he seemed to clash with the horse which was going up while he was going down or visa versa. Although it wasn't quite so bad once they reached the highway, he decided that riding on the rump of a horse was not the graceful and appealing vision he remembered from his youth.

Cyric and his men proceeded with boldness once they reached the road for their disguise prevented any inquiries regarding their business or destination.

Willet noticed that there were more people on the road than normal. Instead of an occasional merchant wagon, there were groups of families carrying bundles or pushing carts with their possessions. The behavior of these groups was rather odd as they fled like deer into the surrounding forest at the sight of the knights and then reappeared once they were almost out of sight.

At regular intervals along the road, notices were posted on trees or fence posts. After passing several of them, Cyric halted the column, pulled one off a tree and read aloud.

By Royal Proclamation of His Highness
King Vulpes of Meglondon
Be it made known that
The Once and Forever Ruler
is henceforth decreed to be the only true faith.
All loyal subjects shall immediately swear by it
and adhere to it alone.
Anyone refusing to do so is considered a traitor
and their possessions and lives are hereby
declared to be forfeit.

"Mayhem and madness!" exclaimed Willet.

Camlin replied, "Aye! This is nothing less than official permission to persecute anyone who does not accept *The Once and Forever Ruler.*"

Willet sadly said, "It is the end of the world we know and the beginning of chaos and war!"

Thereafter, they rode with greater haste and urgency fueled by fear of what might await them as the mayhem spread. Smoke rising from the forest before them caused Cyric to halt their progress.

Oriana asked, "Why do we stop?"

Cyric replied, "Ahead where the smoke rises is the village of Kilkenny. This road takes us through it and is the shortest route to Camlin. However, I do not like the looks of yonder smoke. It may be best to go around through the forest."

Oriana's eyes blazed as she scoffed, "Do you forget who

you appear to be? You are the King's knights! If there is injustice ahead, you have the power to right it!"

She spurred her horse and forced them to follow her to the village.

At the edge of the village, they stopped at the sight of the horror before them. A man, woman and young girl hung from a large branch of an oak tree. On the chest of each of them was a piece of paper that said, "TRAITOR."

Cyric slowly shook his head and said, "That was the mayor and his family."

Oriana was dumbfounded but Tom was indignant and said, "Who would do such a terrible thing?"

Willet sighed, "Those who are zealous to prove their allegiance to the new order view such acts as necessary to purify and unite mankind. They can justify any evil if it advances the cause of their beliefs."

Tom said, "I don't understand how men can believe that evil can bring about good."

Willet looked at him with sadness and gently said, "You are pure of heart and have grown up protected from the deceptions and schemes of the enemy. However, I fear that you will soon be exposed to them."

Oriana suddenly shouted, "We must make haste to do what we can to save others from such violence!"

Cyric waved his arm and the troop continued at a gallop through the deserted streets. They headed towards the rising smoke that appeared to come from the center of Kilkenny. Here and there they noticed houses that had been looted. The front doors and windows were broken and some of their contents were strewn on the street. The word "TRAITOR" was painted on these houses.

A few blocks from the village center the street was filled with people who were shouting, "No book but one! No prophet but Andhun!"

Armed with farm implements, meat cleavers and knives they crowded towards the rising smoke and so did not see the advancing troop of knights behind them.

"Make way for the king's men!" shouted Cyric as they reached the crowd. They slowed to a walk as the crowd parted in layers before them. Most of the villagers either looked surprised or indignant at first but then quickly bowed and respectfully moved aside when they recognized the king's knights. There were hundreds of villagers jammed into the small central square. They continued to shout, "No book but one! No prophet but Andhun!" Cyric had to continually shout to get the attention of those in front of them so that he was nearly hoarse by the time they reached the source of the smoke.

In the center of the village square, there was a raised platform. On one side of it was a huge bonfire that was being fueled by books that the villagers threw into it as they filed past. Near the bonfire were three wagons filled with solemn and terrified men, women and children. As the villagers filed past the bonfire, they shouted curses or taunted those inside the wagons. Others were busy erecting wooden poles around which more books, chairs and other household items were piled. Some of the people in one of the wagons were being taken out and tied to the wooden poles when Cyric reached the platform.

Cyric and a handful of his men dismounted and calmly climbed the steps up to the platform where the local constable and several other prominent villagers stood. The remainder of the knights rode around the perimeter of the platform and surrounded it while Cyric addressed the constable known as Hockley.

"In the name of King Vulpes, I demand that these traitors be released into my custody!"

The village leaders looked uncertainly towards Hockley who said, "We are carrying out the king's proclamation. Why do you interfere?"

Cyric replied, "I have orders from the king to arrest any traitors in this village and deliver them for interrogation."

As Cyric spoke he kept the visor of his helmet down since he and Hockley had crossed paths before. Hockley sensed something familiar about the voice of this knight and asked, "Let me see your orders."

Cyric walked up to him and raised his visor while he drew his dagger and placed it against Hockley's belly. Cyric's men on the platform followed his lead so that all of the officials found themselves being held at knife point.

Hockley hissed, "Cyric! You snake! I should have known that no true knight would attempt such treachery." He waved towards the prisoners and said, "Scum such as them no doubt appeal to one such as you!"

Cyric jabbed him with his dagger and whispered, "Don't lecture me on treachery for you are a master of it. You are as much a thief as I only you cover your theft with your office. Now, order the prisoners to be released to my custody!"

Cyric and his men walked behind Hockley and the other officials. The crowd parted menacingly before them once they realized who they were. The wagons followed them and last came the mounted knights. Once they left the crowd and were near the edge of the village, Cyric motioned toward

Oriana and said, "This time fortune favors you Hockley. Since we are in the presence of a lady, I am inclined to release you. But beware! If I find you killing or torturing innocent people in the future, I shall not be merciful next time!"

Hockley sneered, "Now I know you have lost your mind! That's no lady! I see noth'in but scum!"

Oriana's face flushed deep red and she shouted, "Silence you impudent dog! I am Oriana, princess of Eisendrath!"

"Hah! More likely touched in the head I'd say!"

Cyric said, "Be on your way before I change my mind and make an example of you as you have done to the mayor!"

Once they had traveled several miles beyond of Kilkenny, Willet spoke to Oriana. "You must be more discreet and not be so easily provoked into revealing your identity. Now we must hope that Hockley has no doubts that you are touched in the head."

"I am sure nothing will come of it," replied Cyric.

"How can you be so sure?" asked Willet.

"We will soon leave this road and enter the foothills that lead to Camlin. Many have tried to find it unescorted but have failed. Besides, even if it could be found, it is so well defended that we could defeat ten times our number."

Oriana gave Cyric a smile and slight nod to acknowledge his noble defense of her behavior. These gestures irritated Tom who decided that he did not like or trust Cyric.

CAMLIN

*T*HEY SOON LEFT THE ROAD and began to climb into the foothills surrounding Camlin. As they climbed, the forest thinned until they were crossing bare rock invaded by scattered shrubs that anchored themselves in cracks. In contrast to the green forest below, the landscape before them was barren rock that undulated like giant waves. Their passage left no trail and, after crossing several hills, Tom could not tell where they were much less where they were going. Occasionally, he would peer down into a sink hole or a ravine that had trees and grasses surrounding flowing or pooled water.

When the sun reached the horizon, Tom began to worry that they would have to cross this rugged terrain in the dark. Shadows crept into the ravines and were turning from grey to blackness when they descended into one of them. At the bottom, they followed a narrow and winding stream bed filled with trees. Although there was only a trickle of water moving through the cobble stone riverbed, Tom could see evidence of damage to the trees from rushing water following rain events. On either side, there were sheer rock walls that rose beyond his sight in the gathering darkness.

Cyric gave a bird call that was answered by two or three similar calls in the rocks above them on either side. After traveling several hundred more yards, he would give another but different bird call that was again answered from the rocks above. In this manner, they proceeded past what must have been half a dozen check points until the ravine suddenly opened before them to reveal the village of Camlin.

The full moon cast a silver glow that reflected off of the village roof tops. Hundreds of lights spread across the valley floor before them. Wisps of smoke from many chimneys carried the fragrance of food mixed with burning oak and hickory. The village was surrounded by sheer rock walls hundreds of feet high that looked like giant shadows in the moonlight. In front of them was an expanse of water that formed a moat one hundred feet wide. A stone bridge with four towers spanned the water. Lights from each of the tower windows indicated a well guarded drawbridge.

"Welcome to my humble home!" Cyric said to Oriana. "I regret that the hour precludes a proper entrance for such a distinguished guest as yourself. However, I assure you that a warm bath, soft bed and silk clothes shall be yours."

The village was quiet and few people were visible as they approached the drawbridge. Tom heard frogs croaking and a dog barking. He was struck by the peaceful tranquility of Camlin which reminded him of his life long ago in the village of Downs End.

The tranquility was broken by a guard who challenged

them. Once the guard discovered it was Cyric, he began to shout "Cyric has returned!

His shout was picked up by the guards in the other towers and spread through the village. In the time it took for them to cross the drawbridge, the villagers were pouring out of their houses. They lined the street before them holding torches and shouting, "Hail Cyric!"

Cyric waved and nodded in response to the cheers. Some of the mothers ran beside him and lifted their babies to him. Cyric would kiss each one and carefully hand them back to their mothers.

Oriana was impressed by the enthusiasm, warmth and respect shown to Cyric.

"Why do they honor you so?" she asked.

Cyric smiled and said, "They revere me as their sovereign Lord for I have rescued them from the tyranny of King Vulpes. I have provided a better life for them here."

Willet added, "There is more than you have said."

In response to Oriana's questioning gaze Cyric replied, "Willet is correct, I am also of royal blood for I am the son of King Vulpes!"

Tom and Oriana were dumbfounded and nothing more was said until they arrived at a large hall in the center of the village. As they moved slowly through the crowd, they continued to cheer and shout, "Hail Cyric!"

They dismounted and ascended the stairs to the hall. When they reached the top of the staircase, Cyric turned and addressed the crowd.

"Dear friends, my heart leaps for joy at our reunion! However, my heart is also heavy as I bring you grievous news of persecution resulting from a recent proclamation of King Vulpes."

At the mention of the king's name, the crowd began to hiss and boo until Cyric raised his hands for silence. Pointing to the wagons he said, "Please welcome these gentle folk from Kilkenny! They, like many of you, have come here with nothing seeking shelter. Please care for them as your new brethren!"

"It is our privilege to serve them!" shouted the crowd.

Cyric continued, "It is now my honor to introduce to you three distinguished guests of mine." He took Oriana by the hand, raised it above their heads and shouted, "Hail Oriana, Princess of Eisendrath!"

The crowd responded by repeating Cyric's words and cheering until he repeated the introduction of Willet and then Tom in similar fashion. After he introduced Tom, there was a scream and a woman emerged from the crowd.

"Tom! Tom!" she shouted as she ran towards them.

"Mother? Is that you?" Tom cried and he rushed down the staircase to embrace his mother.

COUNCIL OF THIEVES

*C*YRIC CALLED AN EMERGENCY SESSION of the council as soon as they arrived. Consequently, several hours later every seat in the meeting hall was filled when Tom, Willet and Oriana returned to the entrance. They had bathed, eaten and changed clothes in preparation for this special meeting.

The great hall was filled with the fragrance of cedar. Two rows of massive wooden pillars ran from the back to the front of the large rectangular hall. At the end opposite the entrance, there was a "U" shaped table and chairs. Cyric sat in the center seat with a dozen village elders on each side. Before them were three empty chairs in the center of the "U" shaped table. The villagers were seated on rows of wooden benches that ran the length of the chamber on either side except for a center aisle.

Oriana was stunning in a long red silk gown embroidered with pearls. Her necklace glittered in the torchlight that reflected off of the multi-colored stones on her chest. She wore a gold crown fit for a queen that was inlaid with dozens of diamonds. When they appeared at the entrance opposite the council chamber table, a hush came over the crowd.

Everyone stood as the doorkeeper announced, "Her royal majesty the Princess Oriana of Eisendrath!"

Oriana advanced with the dignity and regal bearing she assumed for important public appearances.

Willet and Tom followed her like a shadow. It was apparent that they were invisible to the assembly. The doorkeeper, like everyone else, seemed captivated by Oriana's beauty and forgot to announce them.

At the far end of the hall, Cyric and the village elders stood at their places behind the great table. When they reached the table, they descended two steps into the sunken area surrounded by the council table. Oriana took the center seat with Willet and Tom on either side. Once they were seated, Cyric took his seat which was directly across the table from Oriana. The elders then took their seats followed by the rest of the assembly.

Cyric beamed with delight at Oriana and said, "Your presence is like a bright star whose radiance dims all others! We are honored to have such royal beauty grace this hall!"

"Here! Here!" shouted the assembly in response.

Cyric took the crown from the table before him and placed it on his head. He nodded to the elders on either side and said, "This council is now in session. The matter before us will be pleaded by Willet."

Willet rose and, after slowly bowing to the elders, he addressed them and said, "We are here to humbly seek your help in defeating King Vulpes and those who support the brotherhood of Andhun."

Willet recounted their rescue of Oriana (without mentioning

how they arrived or how they found her), Andhun's plans to crush the three kings who oppose him, the victory of King Torin and their mission to convince King Alric of Strathyre to join King Torin in marching to the aid of Lochlemond.

While Willet was speaking, Tom felt that something was wrong. At first, he tried to dismiss it as illogical given the hospitality and respect shown them. When he felt a familiar burning sensation on his chest and became aware of the weight of the invisible stone, he ceased doubting and submitted to its guidance. As he looked around, he did not see anything unusual until his gaze fell on the elder called Haggert who sat to the left of Cyric.

Tom blinked and then rubbed his eyes in an attempt to clear his vision. Above Hagget's head there hovered a large, formless shadow that Tom thought must be due to the torchlight. However, as he stared at it, the shadow gradually grew darker and took shape. Tom shuddered as the black shadow transformed into a large demon who stared maliciously at him.

Willet concluded by saying, "Therefore, we humbly seek your assistance in reaching King Alric as soon as possible."

Cyric looked around and said, "What say you? We are at a cross road. The world around us is changing and a new order is displacing the old. What shall our course be?"

Tom saw the demon whisper into Haggert's ear.

"Thieves we are and always shall be!" shouted Haggert. "Why should we care if one tyrant replaces another? They are all our enemies!"

Willet replied, "Not all kings are tyrants nor will all kings treat you as thieves if you now come to their aid in this time of need."

Tom noticed that Haggert glared at Willet with the same expression as the demon looked at him.

Haggert clentched his fists and pounded on the table as he rose from his seat.

"Who is this old man? A beggar who would destroy us by joining a lost cause! I say we should look after ourselves! This conflict could be to our advantage since the king's men are off fighting others instead of seeking us."

Oriana gripped the arms of her chair while Haggert spoke. When he paused she said, "Your survival depends on the prosperity of others. The chaos we saw in Kilkenny is doubtless spreading into other villages. The result will be that there will be no fat sheep for you to sheer for months or years to come!"

Haggert was not used to being lectured before the council and reacted angrily to Oriana's words.

"Fancy words from a fancy figure!" sneered Haggert. "It is high and mighty types like you who think they are better than others that have driven us to live like thieves!"

Tom felt a surge of energy deep inside that caused him to rise from his seat and approach Haggert. He drew his sword and pointed it at Haggert's face. He tried to remain calm but his hands trembled as he heard himself say, "You have insulted my lady and have poisoned this council with your presence long enough! Come forth and let us settle this matter by combat! Let him whose cause is best prevail!"

Haggert started to withdraw his sword but Cyric restrained him and shouted, "So be it! Our course shall be decided by combat! However, I will not have this council hall turned into an arena! Haggert and Tom shall settle this matter outside!"

Trial By Torchlight

*T*HE COUNCIL HALL EMPTIED INTO an adjacent courtyard where they formed a circle about fifty feet in diameter. Torches mounted into stands in the cobblestone pavement outlined the circle. Willet and Oriana stood beside Cyric and the elders while Tom and Haggert stood at opposite ends of the circle. A hush came over the crowd as Cyric raised his sword above his head.

"As is our custom, a challenge has been issued by Tom to settle the choice before the council by combat. Therefore, Haggert shall choose the weapons."

Haggert replied, "Swords and daggers!"

"So be it!" ordered Cyric. "This combat shall end when someone yields or is vanquished."

While Cyric addressed the crowd, Tom wondered how he had gotten himself into this predicament. He didn't know the customs of this people yet he had acted as though he did. After he had issued the challenge and it was accepted, he felt the surge of energy that led him to act so impulsively subside. Looking across the ring, he seemed to see Haggert for the first time and realized that he had challenged one of the strongest and best warriors in the village. Haggert stood a head taller than Tom and was a seasoned warrior who had fought his way to a place of honor beside Cyric. Not only was Haggert physically imposing but Tom could see that the demon associated with him undoubtedly increased his fighting abilities.

After the challenge, Tom and Haggert were escorted immediately outside so that Tom could not seek Willet's advice. As he looked at Willet, he saw an expression of hopeful concern on his face like a father worried for the safety of his son. Their eyes locked briefly and they exchanged slight nervous smiles. Tom looked at Haggert who leered at him like a tiger about to pounce on its prey. The demon stood on Haggert's shoulders and snarled at Tom before sinking into Haggert's body. Once inside, Tom could see the red, cat-like eyes of the demon focused on him.

As they faced each other waiting for Cyric to announce the start of the fight, Tom felt some pressure on his shoulders. Looking up he saw the elf lord Egric looking down at him.

He smiled at Tom with confidence and said, "Do not be dismayed for I am with you!"

Tom raised his arms and cried, "Egric!"

Cyric said, "Look! He must be calling to his god!"

Oriana turned towards Willet to ask him a question but stopped short when she saw that his arms were raised like Tom. His eyes were shut and his lips were moving but no words came out. Cyric also looked at Willet and shrugged his shoulders at Oriana.

"Let the combat begin!" he shouted.

Tom and Haggert met in the center of the circle. The clashing sound of swords and daggers resounded in rapid succession as they slashed, paried and lunged at each other. The ferocity and strength of Haggert were matched by the agility and skill of Tom. They circled round and round the ring in a deadly dance the like of which the crowd had never seen before. From the moment that Egric had been joined to him, Tom's senses and reflexes were magnified. He found himself performing martial arts movements that his mind told him he did not know. However, he executed them instinctively so that he did not think about what he was going to do next. Occasionally, he would hear Egric's voice in his head giving instructions or encouragement. However, for the most part, the action moved too fast for him to focus on what must have been lightening communications at the speed of thoughts.

After thirty minutes of intense but indecisive fighting, they were soaked with sweat and blood. They had both been cut in various places but neither had been able to land a serious blow. They separated and stood at opposite ends of the circle gasping for air.

As they paused, Cyric asked, "Do either of you yield?"

"Nay!" replied Tom.

Everyone looked at Haggert for his response. Saliva drooled from his mouth and his eyes rolled upwards showing only the whites of his eyes. He began to tremble with convulsions as he spoke with an unnatural, hissing voice, "STOOOONNNE! Give us the STOOOONNE!"

A shocked silence followed until Cyric repeated the question. "Haggert, do you yield?"

Haggert suddenly stopped shaking and appeared to return to himself. He looked at Tom and said, "It's time to end this! Submit and give us what we want or die!"

Tom heard a voice in his head say, "Run!" As he started to run, he saw Haggert running towards him and then he felt himself jumping to meet him. Both of them raised their swords and swung them down while swinging their daggers in a slashing motion across the mid-section. They met in mid-jump in the center of the circle. Tom's sword broke in half and their daggers interlocked a fraction of a second before their bodies collided. Tom saw an explosion of light and then lost consciousness as his head smashed into Haggert's.

Tom felt a throbbing pain in his head and, when he opened his eyes, he saw Haggert crawling towards his sword. A voice in his head urged him to roll over. When he rolled over, he felt his dagger beneath him. He slowly got up while struggling against his swirling vision. Haggert recovered his sword and dagger and then turned to face Tom. Although dazed, Haggert had recovered more quickly than Tom and now had the advantage of sword against dagger.

A look of triumph appeared on Haggert's face as he realized his advantage. The smile on Haggert's face dissolved when the voice in Tom's head prompted him to say, "This is your last chance to yield and live!"

"Come and meet your doom!" sneered Haggert as he beckoned Tom to attack.

Tom's vision suddenly cleared and he heard Egric say, "Attack and leave the rest to me!"

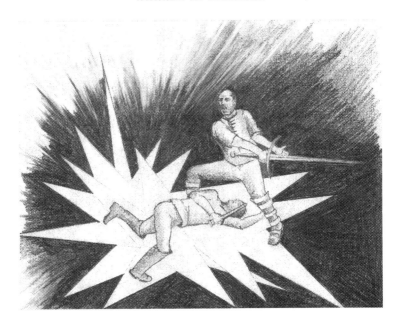

Once again Tom ran towards Haggert who stood his ground. Just before they met, Tom saw Haggert's sword slicing towards his face. He dove below the blade and rolled between Haggert's legs. When Haggert turned, he met the point of Tom's dagger which penetrated his heart.

Haggert's body convulsed like a rag doll and he dropped his weapons. An unnatural howl came from his mouth as he fell dead at Tom's feet. The crowd slowly converged on them until Cyric proclaimed, "By virtue of combat, a new course has been decided. Henceforth, we shall no longer be called thieves but patriots in the cause of *The Past and Future King!*"

THE ROAD TO STRATHYRE

*E*ARLY THE NEXT MORNING, TOM prepared his horse for the journey to see King Alric of Strathyre. Although Cyric provided them with horses, supplies and even an escort, Tom still harbored ill feelings towards him.

"Leaving so soon?"

Tom turned and saw his mother walking towards him. He felt guilty that he had not spent more time with her but their late arrival the previous night and their need to reach King Alric as soon as possible prevented it.

"Mother! Please forgive me for this hasty departure!"

His mother smiled and said, "No need to apologize since we will have plenty of time together on the way to Strathyre."

Tom shook his head in disbelief before saying, "As much as I would welcome the time together, this trip is too dangerous."

Cyric, who was tending his mount nearby, overheard their conversation. He approached and said, "Do not be too hasty to dismiss your mother's offer. She has trained in the martial arts for the past two years and is quite able to defend herself."

His mother smiled and nodded to Cyric her appreciation for his compliment.

Cyric continued, "In Camlin, every man, woman and child who are able and willing train regularly in the martial arts."

"It gives us an advantage in setting ambushes since the king's knights do not consider women and children capable of wielding weapons," added his mother.

Cyric replied, "I pray that you will not have to demonstrate your skills before meeting King Alric." He paused and stared down the village street as if he were already far away. After a moment, his eyes returned to them and he said, "Our paths must part for now. I go to enlist support from other villages similar to Camlin. You should have no trouble until you reach the border of Strathyre as you will be escorted by thirty of the best knights of King Vulpes!"

As if in response, Tom heard a low rumbling sound that quickly grew louder until he saw a column of mounted knights turn onto the village street and approach them. He could see the banners of King Vulpes on their lances.

"Behold your escort! Farewell until we meet again! I go to take my leave of fair Oriana and that old scoundrel Willet."

As Tom watched Cyric walk over to Oriana and Willet, his mother said, "She's a bit skinny and head strong but I believe she's a good match for you!"

Tom could feel the blood rush to his face as he said, "Oriana and I are recent friends and no more. She's high born and too different from me in her thoughts, manners and dreams."

His mother smiled and said, "Nevertheless, she has her eye on you!"

Tom started to object when he looked at Oriana. Their eyes met briefly while she and Willet said farewell to Cyric. In that moment, he saw her briefly smile at him and his heart pounded wildly as he recognized what was so obvious to his mother.

They rode hard until mid-day and then slowed to a walk to allow their horses to recover. Tom and Willet rode beside each other but, due to their pace, they had exchanged only a few words since leaving Camlin. Oriana rode ahead of them beside his mother Heidi who was dressed as one of the king's knights. Ahead of them rode one of Cyric's lieutenants named Ian who was chosen by Cyric to guide them.

"She rides so effortlessly and is so graceful," Tom thought as he watched Oriana move in unison with her mount. Unlike the others, she rode side saddle as she wore a long, green velvet gown. The sun glittered off of the same crown she wore the previous night. They appeared to be the escort of a princess on urgent business in the service of King Vulpes.

Tom's aching bottom reminded him that he had much to learn about riding horses. Soon after they slowed, Ian led them off the road and onto a dirt path that took them to a small spring pond in the forest.

"We shall rest the horses and take our meal here," Ian announced as he dismounted.

Willet helped Oriana down from her mount while Heidi rode over to Tom and said, "Come with me! It is time we get reacquainted!"

Although Tom ached to get off of his horse, he followed his mother a short distance around the pond where they could see the others but not be overheard. Heidi dismounted and raised her visor as she said, "My heart aches to know you better. There is so much to say yet there seems to be so little time for us to share! I hope you will humor me in stealing you from the others so that we can have this time to ourselves," she said as she dismounted and removed her helmet.

Tom dismounted and walked over to her, placed his hands on her cheeks and gazed into her green eyes. He stared fondly at her and gently rubbed her cheeks as he wondered at the changes that the years had made. Gone was the self assured and strong willed young woman that he had known. There was a new source of strength in her that was deeper than her appearance. He could sense it but could not yet define it.

Heidi placed her hands on his face and tenderly said, "Am I so different to you that you look at me so!"

"Much has changed!" replied Tom.

"Yet much remains the same!" said Heidi. "You are still the joy of my life!" Tears welled up in her eyes as she said, "I feel great loss at the years we have been parted but I also feel great joy to see the fine young man you have become! Yes, much has changed and yet my love for you remains!"

Heidi removed her hands and said, "Come! Sit and eat while I tell you how I have become as you see me." She took a blanket and the saddle bag from her horse and spread the blanket on the grass near the pond.

Tom sat beside her and absent mindedly munched on some salted pork and potatoes while she told her story.

"After your sudden disappearance, we never gave up hope that you were alive. Willet also disappeared at the same time and this encouraged us to believe that you were in his care. At first, we continued to go through the motions of our daily routines much as if you were with us but they seemed meaningless without you. Throm blamed himself for your disappearance. He told me that he had forbidden you from reading any more fantasy books shortly before your disappearance. He confessed that he had hidden a copy of *The Past and Future* King in the barn and had shown it to you. This revelation opened an old wound between us and he seemed to emotionally withdraw from me.

As the years passed, he began to have nightmares and he would sometimes wake up screaming your name. He stopped working and would just sit and cry or stare out the window. He began to talk to you as though you were still with us. Needless to say, our friends and neighbors thought he was loosing his mind. Heidi paused and sobbed quietly before she composed herself and continued.

The farm gradually fell apart despite my efforts to keep it going. Eventually, I sold the livestock and everything else of value to survive. It was not long thereafter that I was visited by some poor town folk who were members of a secret brotherhood of thieves. They said that they were mostly farmers like me that had fallen on hard times. Since I saw no other choice, I agreed to join them. Thereafter, I would sneak away one or two nights a week to raid the country side. They taught me how to steal valuables without being detected. I learned how to set an ambush and I was trained in the martial arts. We disguised ourselves and stole only from the wealthy and never more than they could afford. Our success eventually drew the attention of King Vulpes who dispatched some of his knights to capture us but they were unsuccessful.

One night I awoke to find Throm talking to a dark and empty room. He claimed that you and Willet were there." She paused and looked at Tom with a searching gaze that made him uncomfortable. "Of course that's not possible, is it?

Tom looked away but said nothing as she continued, "Throm believed that you told him to go to the enchanted lake and jump in." She sensed his discomfort and paused again.

Tom forced himself to look at her and tried to innocently ask, "What happened?"

Tears again welled up in her eyes and she sobbed, "I begged him not to jump but he said something about knowing the truth." She swallowed and wiped the tears from her eyes, "He looked at me and I saw peace and joy in his face as I had not seen for many years. He told me he loved me and then jumped into the lake and I lost him."

Tom's vision blurred and he wiped the tears from his eyes. He felt her loss and was filled with compassion. There was a warm sensation in his chest and he felt a familiar weight around his neck. He cupped his hands around one his mother's ears and whispered, "Do not fear! Have faith! It is not the end but the beginning!"

Heidi began to tremble when she heard these words which were last spoken in her mind many years before. She went limp and Tom caught her. When she opened her eyes, she looked deep into his and whispered, "You! How can this be!"

Tom looked at her tenderly and said, "With faith, many things that seem impossible can be realized."

At the mention of the word "faith," she stopped trembling and seemed to gather herself. "I have ever hoped for a better tomorrow and have found strength to endure each day alone by believing that you were alive and that I would again see you!"

Tom smiled and said, "Faith is believing in what is unseen and acting as though it is seen!"

Heidi smiled and Tom thought she looked more like a child than his mother. She beamed at him with joy and what seemed to Tom like relief that her faith in their reunion had come to pass.

She soon composed herself and continued, "After Throm left, I no longer felt at home on our farm and soon sold it. I felt guilt and shame for how I had driven both of you to be successful farmers. What seemed so important became meaningless to me and I longed to escape from my past. I heard of a place called Camlin where I heard it was possible to begin a new life without being judged by the past. She smiled at him and said, "Now you know my story. I would like to hear yours but I see Ian waving for us to return."

Tom felt relieved that he had more time to consider what he would tell her. Her faith had given her strength and had helped her redefine her life. However, Tom wondered if she had enough faith to accept the whole truth.

STRANGE SIGHT

$\mathcal{T}$OM FELT UNEASY AS HE and his mother rejoined the others. At first, he thought it was just his imagination but, as they got close, his heart started to race. While the others were mounting up and reforming ranks, Oriana sat motionless and majestic on her horse. She stared intently in his direction. Tom's palms started to sweat and his throat tightened and became dry. "Could she be staring at me because she likes me?" he thought as he tried to look calm.

He forced himself to look about but his eyes were drawn back to her. Everyone else seemed out of focus. He felt a surge of nervous excitement whenever he looked away and then back to her. "She must be looking at me!" he decided as he rode up to where she sat.

"How beautiful she is!" he thought as he stared at her golden hair, light blue eyes, fair skin and shapely figure. Their eyes seemed to lock onto each other.

A slight smile suddenly appeared on her face which made Tom feel suddenly warm as he blushed in response. He felt awkward as he returned her smile. He quickly looked away as he rode past because he did not know what to do or say. Tom was both thrilled and scared by their brief moment of visual contact. As he maneuvered his horse back into position behind her, he criticized himself for not seizing the moment.

"Cyric would have said something eloquent to charm her," he thought. "Why do I feel my throat tighten to strangle my voice and my mind go blank when I have the chance to impress her?"

"Forward!" shouted Ian and they resumed their journey at a quick gallop.

Tom replayed the scene with Oriana over and over in his mind as he thought of how he should or might have acted to impress her. His thoughts were soon interrupted by Willet who pointed ahead and shouted, "More refugees!"

Several hundred yards ahead of them Tom could see a dozen figures scatter in various directions into the surrounding forest. They abandoned their things as they fled leaving several wagons and baggage scattered on the road.

When they reached the spot, Ian raised his hand and shouted, "Column halt!" He reined his mount to a hard stop which set off a chain reaction. Tom desperately pulled back on his reins but, even as he did so, he realized that his riding skills were inadequate. His mount bumped into Oriana's horse and he felt sick to his stomach as he left his saddle and pitched over the head of his horse. Time seemed to slow down as he crashed into Oriana's back and saw her fall before him. He tried to straighten his arms to keep his weight from landing on her. Fortunately, he knocked her into a straw filled wagon so that the only thing that was broken was his pride. Tom panicked and stopped breathing as he got off of her and rolled her over. Her eyes were closed and she was limp and unconscious.

"Oriana! Please wake up!" he pleaded as he gently shook her.

Oriana slowly opened her eyes. Her head was spinning and her vision was blurred. When her vision cleared, she saw Tom's worried face looking down at her. As she struggled to remember what happened, she focused on his eyes and seemed to look deep into his soul. She sensed how deeply he cared for her and his concern made her feel warm and secure. She thought she must be loosing consciousness again as Tom's face faded and a wonderful light seemed to engulf her and caress her. She experienced a brief moment of intense joy and peace that passed like a crashing wave revealing Tom's face.

She smiled at Tom who was covered in straw and said, "You sure make a handsome scarecrow!"

Tom's relief was quickly overwhelmed by his embarrassment as he realized what he had done. He quickly got off of her and helped her to her feet. Oriana steadied herself and then started to laugh as she figured out what happened. When the others saw they were all right, they relaxed and joined in the laughter which became contagious.

A strange voice interrupted their laughter.

"Hail your majesty! Have mercy upon me!"

Tom turned to see a thin old man kneeling in the middle of the dirt road not ten feet from Ian's horse. His clothes were tattered and soiled. He clutched a walking stick to his chest with one hand and raised the other as he pleaded.

"Please forgive this worthless old man for being so bold but I have never been this close to nobility!" He began to crawl on his knees towards them swinging his stick from side to side.

"He's blind!" whispered Oriana as she extended her hand towards the old man so that he might kiss it. Much to her surprise, the old man crawled past her and wrapped his arms around Tom's feet kissing them as he began to weep.

"My lord, please forgive my boldness but never have I experienced such majesty and power among men! You must be a great nobleman or king!"

Tom was dumbfounded and didn't know what to say or do. An embarrassing silence ensued during which Oriana first felt slighted and then amused by Tom's predicament. She quickly looked about and saw open mouths and blank stares that reflected her initial reaction. However, when she looked at Willet she saw that he was smiling and nodding slightly as if in agreement. When he noticed that Oriana was looking at him, he quickly assumed a surprised look but not before she saw his approval of the blind mans' behavior.

Ian dismounted and rushed over to the old man saying, "He's not only blind but crazy as well! We'll suffer no more delay from his strange ravings!"

He started to grab the old man by the back of his tunic which caused him to cling tighter to Tom's feet.

The old man screamed, "Master! Please don't let me be parted from you!"

Tom felt compassion for him and waved Ian away. "Let him be! Can't you see he's blind and needs help!"

At the mention of the word "blind" the old man started to chuckle. He looked up at Tom who saw some sort of growths over his eyes.

"Yes, I'm blind as a bat! That's what everyone says! Yet, like a bat, I see but not as men see!"

Ian replied, "He's raving mad!" and resumed pulling him away.

Tom felt a burning sensation in his chest and thought his seeing stone must be glowing but he could not see it. He pushed Ian away and said, "Let him be!" He looked down at the old man and asked, "What is your name?"

Tears welled up in the old man's eyes as he replied, "Kerwin! It has been a long time since anyone cared enough to ask me that question. Since my wife died, I have sold what meager things we had to buy food. When my money ran out, I began to wander and beg to stay alive. Usually I am cursed, ignored or given some scraps or coins to get rid of me because I make others feel guilty."

Tom gently stroked the top of Kerwin's bald head and said, "You may ride with me and share such as I have for as long as you wish."

Kerwin again embraced Tom's feet and kissed them. He raised his hands over his head and looked up as he shouted, "Praise be to the Creator who has delivered this wretch from a lonely and destitute life! He has guided me to a champion among men!" He then looked at Tom and said, "I pledge my life and my gift to your service henceforth!"

"Gift?" asked Tom as he looked at him curiously.

"Yes! Though I am blind to what you see, I can see the spirit realm. The spirits of most men are as blind, miserable and helpless as you see me!" Kerwin smiled and said, "But not you Master! You are exceptional! I shall help you see as I do!"

White Owl Inn

KERWIN WRAPPED HIS ARMS AROUND Tom and hung on as they rode at a rapid gallop. On several more occasions, Tom saw more fugitives but they fled into the forest once they saw the king's knights approaching. After several hours of hard riding, they stopped at a cross road. Tom noticed a black cloud rising above the forest several miles ahead and guessed it must be another village on fire. As if in answer to his thoughts, Ian pointed towards the smoke and said, "Smoke rises from the village of Derry which is on the most direct route. To avoid further trouble, we'll turn here and go around on the less traveled way."

They pressed ahead until well after sunset. The night sky was clear and the stars glittered like diamonds strewn across the heavens. The moon was large and bright reflecting enough light so that everything appeared in shades of silver and grey. The horses were near exhaustion and Tom's bottom felt like one big raw sore.

Much to Tom's relief, they suddenly slowed to a walk and

soon after he saw several lights shining from the dark that outlined a building in the distance. When they got close Tom saw that the building was a roadside inn. It was made of logs built on a low stone and mortar base. The only entrance was through a gate that separated the main lodge from the barn. Ian rode up to the gate and pounded on it until Tom heard someone mumbling within. He heard a sliding sound inside as wooden bar in the door slowly opened to reveal a pair of eyes in a slot in the gate. Ian shouted, "Open for the king's knights!"

In response, the door was unbolted and they entered a courtyard enclosed by buildings. The inn keeper was a portly middle aged man with a grey beard and a pointed knit hat that flopped over to one side of his head. He wore a baggy cotton shirt, large leather apron and his loose fitting trousers which were tucked into leather boots. He raised his lantern to see them better and greeted them by saying, "Welcome noble travelers to the Inn of the White Owl! I am honored by your presence! Please enter and refresh yourselves! Morris, William and Egan! Tend to our guests!" shouted the keeper. In response, several young boys suddenly appeared from the shadows of the surrounding buildings and tended to their horses.

Willet helped Oriana dismount and escorted her into the lodge. Tom dismounted and felt his legs wobble for several steps as he walked towards the entrance to the inn. Kerwin grabbed the end of his tunic and followed him. They passed beneath a white, wooden owl that sat on a perch above the door. After pushing open a large wooden door, they entered the main room of the inn which was warm and inviting. There was a large stone hearth upon which a lamb and several fowl were being slowly roasted on a spit turned by a young girl that Tom thought must be the inn keeper's daughter. Animal heads and hides of various sorts adorned the varnished pine logs that formed the walls and ceiling. Yellow light flickered from the hearth and from numerous candles on the tables. To their left was a long bar behind which were various sized kegs, casks and bottles. Three long wooden tables with simple stools spanned the room.

Five men were seated at the table nearest to the hearth. They were a diverse group of various ages, sizes and races who also dressed differently from each other. One wore a turban and a single loose fitting cotton garment from neck to toes while another had a white cuffed silk shirt, broad brimmed hat with a large white feather and bright red trousers and stockings. There was a bald black man who wore only a leather vest and leopard skin loin cloth. The other two wore head scarves, ear rings and looked like gypsies. A large buxom woman was serving them from a metal tray she held on one hand above her head. They abruptly froze at the appearance of the king's knights who followed Tom into the room but then resumed eating when they realized there was no threat to them.

"Come, sit and eat! There's plenty for all!" shouted the keeper's wife as she waved them to come to the table with the others. Although sitting was the last thing Tom wanted to do, the aroma of roasted meat and fresh baked bread persuaded him to obey so he gingerly sat on the stool next to a dark skinned man with black curly hair who wore the bright red trousers. He had black almond shaped eyes and a large mustache which was twisted and turned up at the ends. He looked Tom up and down, pushed a platter of warm bread towards him and resumed eating.

Tom eagerly helped himself to the bread and other platters of food that were passed around. He was amazed that Kerwin not only helped himself but passed each platter like everyone else. As if sensing Tom's thoughts, Kerwin said, "When it comes to food, the clatter of dishes and smell are my eyes!"

Despite the tasty food and welcoming surroundings, the mood in the room was tense and there was little said while they ate. The strangers occasionally glanced at him which made Tom feel uneasy. They seemed to be evaluating him but quickly looked away when he looked at them.

When they were nearly finished eating, Ian entered the room. He had elected to make sure that the horses were properly tended before eating. As Ian entered the room, the stranger next to Tom jumped to his feet and shouted, "Ian! Bless my soul! Either I've lost my mind and my sight or you're masquerading as one of the king's knights!"

Ian froze and the blood drained from his face. Before he could recover, the stranger hurried across the room and embraced him.

"Trossachs?" asked Ian uncertainly as he pushed him away and studied him at arms length.

"Aye! None other!" said the stranger as he smiled at Ian. "I've lost some hair and added some weight over the years but I'm still the same rogue at heart! How about you?"

An uneasy silence ensued during which Tom could see that Ian was considering what to say. The room was silent as everyone waited for Ian's response. Slowly, a mischievous smile grew on Ian's face and he said, "Once a rogue, ever a rogue!" and clapped Trossachs on the back.

Trossachs replied, "Come lads! These are no more the king's men than we are!" He beckoned for his companions to join him and continued, "Come Banagher and Arless, Dingle and Gort! Come and meet an old friend and let's make new ones!" The tension in the room evaporated and they mingled and got acquainted. The introductions were abruptly interrupted by the Inn Keeper who shouted, "Master Trossachs! It's time for you to earn your supper!"

Trossachs and his companions crossed the room to a group of stacked trunks in one corner. As they opened them, Tom saw that they contained various instruments. Banagher grabbed a flute while Arless began to blow on a set of bag pipes. Dingle took out several sizes of drums which he played with his hands. Gort picked up a lute and adjusted the strings as he strummed them. Trussachs took out a fiddle and started to warm up by playing snippets of several tunes.

While they were warming up, the Inn Keeper yelled, "Let's make room for dancing!"

In response, Ian and several knights picked up the tables and moved them to the outside of the room. Everyone grabbed a stool and took their seats near the walls. They then waited patiently for several more minutes as the musicians continued to warm up.

Trussachs walked over to each of his companions and whispered something. One by one each musician completed warming up until the room was silent. Tom noticed that they smiled and nodded to each other with poised anticipation as Trussachs began to tap his foot on the floor. The room suddenly was filled with the rhythm and pulsing beat of a jig.

The music was energetic and reminded Tom of the festivals of his childhood in Downs End. He closed his eyes and pictured his parents and neighbors dancing. For a few moments, the music enveloped him and stimulated his memories so that he felt he was once again a young lad. When he opened his eyes, he looked around and saw that everyone in the room was tapping their feet and clapping their hands.

He continued to look around the room until his gaze fell upon Oriana. The flickering light from the fireplace behind her cast a golden glow that highlighted her blond hair. As she watched the musicians, Tom studied her face and figure and thought to himself that she was the most beautiful woman he had ever seen. As if sensing his gaze, Oriana suddenly looked at him and smiled. Although she only looked at him briefly, her eyes and smile filled him with conflicting feelings. He sensed that she liked him which caused his heart to beat rapidly and his palms became moist. However, he immediately chastened himself for thinking too much of a casual glance and friendly smile.

As he wrestled with these conflicting thoughts and feelings, he tried to look casually around the room but his gaze was frequently drawn to Oriana. He hoped to catch another smile or look from her that would indicate she was attracted to him.

"Ask her to dance," said his mother as she nudged him in the side. Tom felt his face flush and he became embarrassed that his stolen glances towards Oriana were so easily detected.

Tom looked down at his hands on the table and replied, "I'm afraid. I don't know how to dance."

"That's no excuse! It's easy! I will teach you!" replied his mother.

While Tom considered this offer, the inn keeper and his wife entered the dance floor. Once Tom saw their rapid footwork, twirls and coordinated movements, he decided that there was no way he could dance without looking foolish.

Ian stood and walked over to Oriana. He bowed and extended his hand. She smiled and joined him on the dance floor.

A sinking feeling and tightness in the pit of his stomach hit Tom like a wave as he realized that someone else had taken his place. He tried to appear happy and unconcerned but he no longer enjoyed the music. He felt helpless and dismayed by his inability to dance. He pictured himself in Ian's place and coveted Oriana's smiles as they danced.

The next thing Tom knew he was being pulled from his chair. Heidi grabbed his hands and pulled him out onto the dance floor saying, "Sulking won't solve your woes! Just do as I do!"

Tom stood awkwardly while she demonstrated the basic dance steps which seemed impossibly complicated. The music seemed to fade as the pounding of his heartbeat grew louder in his ears. It became hard for him to breathe and he felt that everyone in the room was watching him.

"Focus on the music! Forget about yourself!" said a familiar voice inside of his head.

"Egric!" whispered Tom.

Warmth spread from his chest throughout his body as Tom felt a surge of energy from his invisible seeing stone. At the same time, he felt his legs suddenly mastered the dance steps and realized that Egric was helping him.

"WHAA HOO!" shouted Heidi as she beamed at him with excitement and pride at his quickness to learn. She stomped her feet more emphatically to the rhythm and the musicians answered by picking up the tempo of the jig.

Tom and Heidi took turns circling each other and then danced back to back. Tom no longer thought of himself but focused on the music and in complimenting the movements of his mother. The faces of those seated around the room faded into a blur. He no longer noticed them except for their occasional shouts and the stomping of their feet. Whenever Tom faced his mother, their eyes would meet and Tom sensed that he was reconnecting with her. Although she was still practically a stranger, Tom saw the love in her eyes and the strength of their relationship. He was filled with joy and knew that there was a bond between them that could not be broken. Love and wonder enveloped him as he looked upon the strange and yet familiar middle aged woman. He realized that he was proud to claim her as his mother!

As they danced around the floor, Tom's attention gradually shifted to Oriana. He began to search for discrete glimpses of her whenever she came into view. The energy and passion of her dancing seemed to energize him. She smiled and frequently laughed which infused him with joy and longing to be the object of her affection. Soon the men and ladies formed two lines and danced facing each other.

"Ladies choice!" shouted Tossachs. In response, the inn keeper's wife suddenly crossed the floor and began to dance with Ian. Heidi moved over towards the inn keeper which left Tom paired with Oriana.

As they faced each other, Oriana smiled at him and gave him a look that challenged and encouraged him. She began to dance with even greater energy which spurred Tom to do the same. In response, the musicians shifted into high gear. Tom complimented Oriana's movements perfectly as they danced at a frenzied pace.

Tom focused on the music and Oriana movements. It took awhile for him to notice that Heidi, Ian, the inn keeper and his wife were standing and clapping as they had joined the others in a circle around the dance floor.

Tom's legs began to ache and sweat rolled down his cheeks but he redoubled his efforts when he saw how Oriana now looked at him. She beamed at him with such pleasure that Tom's heart lept for joy. As they moved in unison, the music enveloped and carried them like an ocean current. It created a powerful sense of intimacy in Tom.

"She is mine and I am hers," he thought as he put his arms around her and felt the warmth of her body beside him.

Tom heard Egric's voice inside his head saying, "Look around!" As he did so, Tom saw the smiles, enthusiasm and participation of everyone in the room. They were clapping, stomping, laughing, shouting and playing instruments as they too were carried along in the powerful flow of the music.

Egric's voice inside his head said, "Music is a mighty force that can unify mankind in a common purpose. Look around! See how it has freed everyone here from their inhibitions and selfish ambitions. They have temporarily become part of something greater than themselves!"

As Tom thought about these words, the music reached a crescendo and crashed like a gigantic wave. When the music suddenly ended, he found himself embracing Oriana and looking deeply into her eyes. The smile on her face slowly faded and she closed her eyes. Tom felt himself drawn to her lips. As their lips gently touched, Tom felt his face flush with excitement. When he backed away and opened his eyes, he realized that everyone in the room was applauding and whistling. Oriana grabbed his hand. They ran from the room and out into the courtyard.

"Follow me!" she yelled as she led him across the courtyard.

She opened the front gate and they walked into the clearing outside the inn. They strolled down the road for several minutes in silence as the heat from their bodies dissipated into the cool night air. The cool evening air felt refreshing and Tom noticed that he could produce a puff of vapor when he drew a deep breathe and exhaled.

Tom stopped and looked up at the starry sky. The full moon had set revealing a vast expanse of stars that looked like glowing dust against the blackness of the night sky.

"You dance well," commented Oriana as she followed Tom's gaze to the plethora of stars that spread across the sky.

Tom felt a surge of warmth in his chest and heard his

heart pounded in his ears as he looked upon Oriana. He suddenly became aware of the softness of her hand and felt uncomfortable being so alone with her.

As their eyes met, she smiled at him and Tom felt a tightness in his throat.

Oriana said, "I find you most intriguing! When you first stepped onto the dance floor, you appeared to be a clumsy beginner." She looked inquisitively at him and continued, "Was that just an act or are you a fast learner?"

"Intriguing!" thought Tom to himself. "Is that all I am to her?"

As Tom struggled with his emotions, Oriana laughed as his face changed expressions.

"Egric!" Tom whispered as if pleading for help.

"Egric indeed!" Oriana replied as she became serious and stared intently at him as if examining him. "I have heard you say that name before during your remarkable victory over Haggert. Who is this Egric? Is he an invisible friend or helper?"

Tom was speechless and didn't know what to do so he shrugged his shoulders and smiled sheepishly.

Oriana frowned and said, "You confuse me! Part of me is drawn to you as if by some unseen force but then I realize that we can never be!"

She looked at him as if pleading for his help to explain her feelings. Tom just continued to stare at her blankly at a loss for words. Oriana continued softly as if speaking to herself, "I have promised to marry only nobility in accordance with my heritage and my father's wishes."

She turned from Tom and hid her face in her hands, "I'm miserable and confused! I wish my father was here!"

As she began to cry, Tom's heart leaped for joy. "She does like me! At least I'm more to her than some curiosity!" he told himself. He wanted to put his arms around her but walked beside her and put his arm around her shoulders.

They stood silently while Tom continued to struggle with what to say.

"Egric, where are you?" he thought to himself.

Oriana stopped crying and looked at him. "Have you nothing to say?" she asked.

"Great Creator please help me!" Tom prayed to himself.

Immediately, he felt the weight and warmth of the invisible seeing stone on his chest. His throat loosened and words began to flow from deep within him.

"What has been does not have to determine what can be, he said."

"What do you mean?" asked Oriana as she looked hopefully at him.

Tom replied, "You and I did not choose our parents, place or time of birth or the way we were raised. This was ordained by forces beyond our knowledge or control."

"Do you mean The Creator?" asked Oriana.

Tom paused and then said, "Ultimately, yes, but there are others through whom The Creator works."

"Like Egric?" asked Oriana as she gazed intently into his eyes.

Tom held her gaze but felt like she was looking deep into his soul. He wondered what she saw or sensed about him.

"What I am trying to say is that we have been brought together in this place and time by the design of The Creator. The kingdoms of this world are in turmoil. The old order of peace and prosperity that has lasted a thousand years has passed. What will take its place has yet to be determined. The armies of light and darkness are gathering. What happens depends on how we adapt to meet the challenges ahead."

Oriana's mouth opened but she was speechless. She looked at him and was puzzled by the strange mixture that she saw in Tom. She thought to herself, "One minute he is as clumsy and dull as a farm boy and the next as wise and confident as a king."

She shook herself out of her pondering and asked, "What do you mean?"

Tom smiled as he saw the conflicting thoughts change the expressions on her face. He replied, "Simply that there is hope."

"Hope?" puzzled Oriana.

"Yes, weeping may endure during the night but joy comes in the morning!" Tom replied as he gazed up at the stars.

Oriana took his hand and looked up as she said, "I pray the coming conflict will be quickly settled. Until then, I will cling to hope and look for the dawning of a new day and better time in this world."

Tom looked at her and smiled, "My dawn has already begun! Since we met, you have brought new purpose and meaning to my life!"

Oriana blushed and pulled him towards the inn. "It's getting late and we should return."

UNEXPECTED ENCOUNTER

*T*RUSSACHS AND HIS MINSTRELS JOINED them the next morning as they resumed their urgent trip to the Kingdom of Strathyre. Trossach's had humbly approached Ian to ask if his band of minstrels could accompany them. Ian accepted their company since they had their own horses and promised not to slow them down. Trossach's bowed and said that they were glad to have such fine company in troublesome times. Tom hoped that the minstrels would play for them but it soon became apparent that this was not going to happen.

The morning of their departure from the White Owl Inn was cold and windy signaling an abrupt change in the seasons. As if in response, Tom noticed that here and there some of the aspens had turned to a golden yellow. By midday, they had returned to the main road and continued to ride hard with infrequent stops. Occasionally, they would see smoke in the distance or baggage strewn about on the road but they did not see anyone.

Ian continued to press ahead relentlessly and insisted that

they avoid contact with any villages or inns. During their infrequent rest stops, he instructed them to stay close together so Tom did not have any opportunities to speak further to Oriana or his mother. At night they slept on the ground without any fires or music. Tom's bottom became so raw that he seemed to feel less pain or perhaps he was getting used to the constant pain. Kerwin offered the only companionship as he rode with Tom. Kerwin told Tom that every living thing glowed with an invisible energy that he could see. As they rode, Kerwin would point out the colors and intensities of what he saw.

"There's an exceptionally happy and healthy tree! Can't you see the bright yellow aura around it?" exclaimed Kerwin as he pointed to an ordinary looking pine tree beside the road.

Tom replied, "It looks like any other pine tree to me."

A short while later Kerwin would shout, "What about that rock over there?"

Tom shrugged his shoulders and said, "Looks like large, granite boulder. I suppose its shape is unique if I looked closely enough at its details. From this distance, I see nothing about it that would make me say it is unique compared to the hundreds of others scattered about in these woods."

"It is obviously different! You must look beyond the surface to see as I see!"

Tom felt uneasy and thought that perhaps Kerwin had lost his mind as well as his sight.

On the afternoon of the third day since their departure from The White Owl Inn, they came upon an abandoned coach beside the road. Kerwin looked over Tom's shoulder and tightened his grip as he said, "Blackness surrounds yonder coach!"

As they rode up beside it, Tom saw a young man in the driver's seat. He was slumped over and appeared to be sleeping. Tom's stomach suddenly tightened into a knot as he realized that the man was not sleeping. The driver was leaning on a broken lance that had gone through his stomach and impaled him to the coach. In the ditch nearby, another man lay face down.

Ian halted the column and dismounted. The man in the ditch was someone of wealth or importance judging by his new shoes, silk stockings and fine clothes. Tom could see that he was a bald and rather portly. When Ian turned him over, it was clear he was dead. His white silk shirt was stained a brownish red and the hilt of a dagger protruded from the center of his chest. A sheet of blood soaked paper was stuck to his chest by the hilt of the dagger.

Ian's face was as white as a sheet as he pulled the paper from the dagger and said with disgust, "It appears that the zealots of Andhun are no respectors of persons of wealth or fame."

Tom recognized the paper as a copy of the proclamation issued by King Vulpes. Ian crumpled the paper and threw it away as he said, "This man was Chadwick, governor of this province and one time friend of King Vulpes."

He bent down and closed Chadwick's eyes. "Once I counted you a foe but now I see that you were a man loyal to your beliefs. Too late have I found you to be a friend." Ian pulled Chadwick's cloak slowly over his head and said, "Sleep friend and forgive us for our haste."

The next day was hot and calm. The sun burned brightly

in a clear sky so that by the afternoon the knights were sweating profusely in their armor. When they reached a clearing in the forest, Ian halted the column. Tom thought this was odd since they had just stopped for lunch an hour before. Willet rode up beside Ian and pointed to the forest on the opposite side of the clearing as he said, "I don't like the look of that."

"Neither do I," replied Ian as he stared across the field. "What do you make of it?"

Willet replied, "Judging by the dust and the birds flying about, I would say that a large party approaches."

While they waited to see what would emerge from the woods, Oriana rode up beside them. Soon the sounds of plodding horses, clattering weapons and creaking wheels could be heard. A column of soldiers emerged from the forest and headed towards them across the field. At the head of the column, a knight carried a green and yellow checked banner with a black boar's head.

"Knights from Strathyre!" shouted Oriana. She started to spur her horse but Ian grabbed the reins.

"Hold! We cannot go charging into the open! Don't forget we appear to be knights in the service of King Vulpes!"

"Ian is right," Willet said. "We will be mistaken for enemies if we ride into the clearing."

Oriana replied, "Let me go alone! I will explain who I am. Certainly, someone among my uncle's knights will acknowledge me."

Willet replied, "In the past, a princess riding alone would not be believed. However, we have few options other than to flee because they will soon be upon us."

Ian nodded his agreement and said to Willet, "We will

stay here while you and Tom accompany Oriana and explain our circumstances."

Oriana rode between Tom and Willet. They slowly trotted into the clearing to give the impression that they were not afraid or in distress. As soon as they entered the clearing, a horn sounded and six horsemen left the column and approached at a gallop. They wore yellow and green checked kilts with leather boots to their knees and iron breast plate armor. Their hair was braided and tied behind their heads. Each carried an oval shield with a bore's head and javelins.

As they drew near, Tom sensed that something was not right. As if acknowledging what Tom sensed, Kerwin whispered into his ear, "Something is very wrong with yonder group of men." Before Tom could ask him what he meant, the six knights were upon them.

"Stand and identify yourselves!" demanded the lead horseman who appeared to be in charge. He had a thick, rusty brown beard that covered his face except for his large round nose. His bushy eye brows partly hid his green piercing eyes.

"I am Oriana, daughter of King Thymallis and Princess of Eisendrath!"

At this the men laughed and their leader replied, "Nonsense! Princess Oriana would not be wandering far from her kingdom with such a pathetic looking escort!"

Oriana ignored their disrespect and said, "You are quite right when speaking of what would be customary in times past. However, times have changed. If any of you be noblemen, this should convince you." Oriana held forth her right hand upon which was a gold ring that bore the royal signet of King Thymallis.

The lead horseman examined the ring and his eyes grew

large as he recognized the royal crest. He stopped smiling and looked perplexed as he struggled with whether to believe or not. Seeing his confusion, Oriana said, "Your face confirms that you recognize my claim. However, if any doubts remain examine this!"

Oriana produced a leather pouch from a pocket within her dress. She opened the draw string and took out a gold medallion on a delicate chain. She held it up for all to see.

"This medallion bears the same royal crest but it also bears my image on the back!"

One by one the horsemen dismounted and dropped to one knee as a sign of respect until they all knelt before her.

Oriana said, "Arise and identify yourselves."

The lead horseman replied, "I'm Izora, captain of yonder troop of men-at-arms who were formerly in the service of the King Alric of Strathyre."

"Formerly?" asked Oriana as the blood drained from her face.

Izora's head dropped and he looked embarrassed as he replied in a low voice, "King Alric is dead and we are all that remains of his army."

This news stunned them like a blast of frigid air. Tears welled up in Oriana's eyes and she was at a loss for words. They sat in silence until Willet said, "How did this happen?"

Izora looked sad and dejected. He looked down as he muttered, "King Alric was ill advised by his chief counselor Bournemouth."

"How so?" asked Oriana.

Izora continued, "King Alric refused to submit to Andhun's leadership being a staunch believer in the ways described in *The Past & Future King.* Thus, Andhun sent the armies of

King Ronan and King Whon to conquer us. Their combined armies outnumbered us by more than two to one. Bournemouth persuaded King Alric to ride out and ambush the invaders. A few captains joined me in opposing this course of action but to no avail. Bournemouth persuaded the King to divide his army. King Alric and the main force were to lie in ambush in the wooded Valley of Doune. I was assigned to lead a smaller force behind the invading armies and attack them from the rear after the trap was sprung."

Izora paused and wiped a tear from his eye while his men looked down cast. He cleared his throat and continued, "The only truth to Bournemouth's council was that the Valley of Doune was an excellent place for an ambush. King Alric put Bournemouth in charge during his absence and made haste to the Valley of Doune where he found the invading armies waiting in ambush."

Izora paused again as tears streamed down his face. He clentched his fists as mourning, guilt and anger welled up within him. "King Alric and all the men with him were killed to the last man before we got there. We saw their bodies strewn about in the woods and I came upon King Alric's body when we were attacked. Fortunately, most of the invaders had moved on to claim Alric's throne which I am sure Bournemouth handed to them. Nevertheless, we were still outnumbered and had to fight our way out of the same trap that felled our king."

"How many are with you?" asked Oriana.

"Less than one thousand men," replied Izora. "Every day more of my men disappear to see to their homes or join Andhun's cause."

"Where are you going?" Willet asked.

"We wish to continue to fight but we are too few to face an

army. Therefore, we are seeking a place called Camlin where we have heard that there are many who oppose King Vulpes. We hope to join with those who oppose Andhun and those kings who support him."

Oriana said, "We have come from Camlin and were going to Strathyre to persuade King Alric to march to Lochlemond."

"Why Lochlemond?" asked Izora.

Willet replied, "It is where Andhun's main force will be gathered to deliver a crushing blow to the strongest of the three kingdoms that oppose him."

"You mean two kingdoms," mused Oriana.

"We must make haste to Lochlemond," urged Willet. "Now that Strathyre has fallen, the armies of Kings Ronan and Whon will undoubtedly march to Lochlemond after celebrating with Bournemouth."

Oriana nodded her agreement and said to Izora, "Will you join us?"

Izora smiled and fire flashed in his eyes as he exclaimed, "Aye! We would like another chance to fight those armies that have taken our King and homes. Besides we are men-at-arms and not thieves. A battle is more to our liking than an ambush!"

"Very well," replied Oriana. "Let's make haste to Lochlemond!"

She turned and waved her arm towards the woods behind her whereupon Ian and his troop galloped towards them. Oriana turned back towards Izora with a smile and said, "As you see, although times are changing, this princess still travels with a respectable escort."

DESPERATE FLIGHT

$\mathcal{D}$URING THE NEXT TWO WEEKS, they passed through the Kingdom of Strathyre and entered the Kingdom of Lochlemond. Their pace had slowed since Izora and his men had joined them but they still pressed ahead as fast as the men on foot could go. Their ranks continued to dwindle as Izora's men deserted for home or other pursuits. Izora made no attempt to stop them as he said, "Better to face those who are disloyal as enemies than have them stab me in the back." Nevertheless, he insisted that any who chose to leave do so on foot and posted loyal horsemen around their perimeter. He did not want any word of their plans to find their way ahead of them.

At first, Tom was glad for the slower pace which made riding much more bearable on his sore bottom. However, as the days passed, a sense of urgency slowly grew within him. Tom thought it was just his nerves until he noticed that Willet was unusually quiet and edgy. Also, Kerwin's cheerful demeanor changed and he became fearful of evil shadows and complained about a darkness that grew as they got closer to Lochlemond. Once or twice Tom thought that he too saw the evil shadows that Kerwin pointed out. Soon his sense of urgency was accompanied by a feeling that something dreadful was about to happen.

When they were still several days from their destination, Willet sat beside Tom while he was eating dinner and whispered in his ear, "Something is amiss in Lochlemond. Tonight we must see what it is."

Tom felt a mixture of excitement and fear as he nodded and tried to look calm. After supper, Tom waited until it was dark and slipped away unnoticed when everyone was preparing for sleep. He found a secluded spot a short distance from the camp and unrolled his blanket. Tom had just laid down when Willet joined him and soon they were moving as spirits towards Lochlemond.

Oriana and Heidi were unpacking their bed rolls when Heidi asked, "Have you seen Tom?"

Oriana looked around and replied, "It appears that both Tom and Willet are missing."

"That's odd," said Heidi. "Their horses are also gone. Do you think that they could be riding about?"

"Not likely," replied Oriana as she suddenly became suspicious about what they were doing.

Heidi noticed Kerwin sleeping nearby and said, "Look! Another oddity! Yonder lies Kerwin who never sleeps far from Tom. Let's find out what's happening."

Together they walked silently over to Kerwin who was

restlessly tossing about in a vain attempt to sleep. They stooped over him and Oriana whispered "Kerwin! Awake!"

Kerwin rolled over towards them and said, "Would that I were asleep so I could awake! Is there anything amiss?"

Oriana asked, "Where are Tom and Willet?"

Kerwin's brow wrinkled and his mouth twisted from side to side as he struggled with what to say.

Heidi noticed his anguish and said, "Tom told you not to tell anyone where he went. Isn't that right?"

Kerwin nodded his head yes.

"As his mother, I am not just anyone but someone very special. Therefore, you may tell me."

Kerwin's face brightened as he replied, "Surely Tom did not mean for me not to tell you since a son must not keep secrets from his mother. However, if I tell you, I must be allowed to go with you."

Heidi looked at Oriana who nodded her agreement.

"Very well. Tell us where Tom is."

Kerwin got up and led them in the direction that he sensed Tom had gone. "Tom said that he was going to sleep in the woods at the edge of our camp."

Even in the dark, it did not take long for them to locate their horses which were tied to some trees well beyond where the rest were sleeping. They moved silently through the night a short distance into the woods where they found two shadows lying on the ground. Heidi was the first to reach them. As she knelt down to rouse Tom, she suddenly jumped back in shock and screamed "Tom! No! Please!" She began to cry uncontrollably as she threw herself onto Tom's motionless body.

Kerwin froze and stared in disbelief while Oriana knelt

beside Heidi and placed her hand near his mouth. A slight smile appeared on her face and then she looked serious as she said, "SSHH! You'll alarm the rest of the camp! Tom isn't dead! I've seen this condition before. He is in some sort of trance."

Heidi stopped sobbing and looked dumbfounded as she asked, "Are you sure?

"Yes," replied Oriana. "Look at Willet. I'll wager that you will see the same vacant stare on his face."

Heidi went over to Willet and bent over him. She returned to Oriana both relieved and curious as she said, "It is as you say. What does this mean?"

Kerwin dropped to his knees and began to shake Tom's body.

"His spirit is gone but there is still a slight glow of energy that tells me that he is not dead."

"Leave him be!" ordered Oriana. "Do not touch him!"

She commanded them to sit nearby and wait.

"Will they be alright?" asked Heidi.

"They are as well as two magicians can be who are meditating."

Heidi looked at her incredulously and said, "Magicians?"

"So they have said," replied Oriana with a smug smile. "But this time we shall learn more of this."

Willet and Tom flew beside each other at tremendous speed. It took only a matter of minutes to reach Lochlemond. As they drew near, a vast expanse of water appeared on their left. Tom saw thousands of pin points of light that marked the extent of the city. The forest beneath them abruptly ended and they flew over a wide grass plain bisected by a silver ribbon of water.

Willet signaled to slow down and said, "Yonder lies Lochlemond! A pearl among the cities of the earth! She is a great center of trade sitting at the mouth of the Dileas River and the Capacian Sea. Lochlemond is an ancient and proud city that has grown over hundreds of years to become two in one."

As they flew over the Dileas River, the pin points of light became ramparts and buildings inside of a continuous stone wall.

"We will go through the sea gate," said Willet as he pointed to a massive stone arch with iron bars between two towers. "The founders of this city dug a channel from the Dileas River to an adjacent lake and enclosed it within the stone wall you see."

They flew low over the water and followed the channel to the sea gate. Although it was closed, they passed through its thick iron bars. Tom noticed a sentry leaning heavily on his spear and guessed he must be sleeping. Inside the gate was a large lake that served as a harbor. It was filled with many ships of every imaginable size and shape.

"Below you will find men from all the kingdoms of this earth," said Willet as they passed over the ships.

Willet pointed ahead to the far side of the harbor and said, "The oldest part of the city surrounds this harbor while the rest rises above it."

Before them the city lights spread out along the far shore of the harbor. When they reached them, Tom noticed that they ended abruptly about a quarter mile from the shore. They continued straight ahead and gradually white limestone cliffs appeared in the blackness before them. When they reached them, Willet lead him straight upwards. At the top of the cliffs, the city continued as if it had been thrust upwards from the rest. Tom paused in amazement at the expanse of lights that extended as far as he could see across a flat plain.

Rising above the sea of lights before them was a great mountain of lights that Willet pointed to and said, "Yonder is the palace of King Hostyn. It seems peaceful but I fear treachery is afoot. Let's make haste!"

As they flew towards the peak of the lights, the palace emerged from the darkness. The pyramid of lights became a cluster of towers and spires of many sizes and shapes.

"Gong! Gong! Gong!"

"Something's wrong!" shouted Willet as they made for the source of the sounds. In a few minutes, they were descending upon the tallest tower of the palace. Tom could see numerous lights moving about in various directions as people scurried about in confusion.

"Follow me!" Willet yelled as he dove towards the courtyard surrounding the top of the tallest tower.

When they reached the stone pavement, Willet made straight for the massive stone wall of the tower. They passed through the tower and into the royal chambers. Inside a corridor they found pandemonium as men-at-arms, nobles and servants ran about in panic and alarm. Just ahead of them, two soldiers were throwing themselves against a large wooden door. Huddled nearby were several women who were crying and holding each other.

After passing right through the soldiers and the wooden door, they paused inside a dark bedroom. Before them was a large canopy bed with white lace curtains. In the bed, Tom saw a young girl who was sleeping. Willet motioned for Tom to approach the bed with him. As they slowly moved towards the bed, Tom was sickened to see a large red stain on the blanket covering the girl.

The door behind them shattered with a loud crack and the soldiers and ladies entered the room. The women rushed to the bed, pulled back the blanket and screamed, "No! Tanya! Please No!"

Willet grabbed Tom by the arm and said, "Come! We must hurry!"

They left the girl's bedroom and passed down the corridor entering several other bedrooms. In each case, they found a member of the royal family murdered while they slept.

"They've killed them all," lamented Willet as they gazed upon the lifeless body of King Hostyn.

"Who would do such a cowardly act?" Tom asked.

"Andhun's assassins!" Willet replied. "I fear there must be traitors among those trusted by the royal family. Only those with access to the royal family could carry out such a complete slaughter without leaving a sign of any struggle or forced entrance."

"What do we do now?"

Willet said, "Nothing more can be done here tonight. We must return to our camp as soon as possible. Without any surviving member of the royal family, there will be a power struggle."

An Awkward Awakening

Tom and Willet returned to their camp to find Oriana, Heidi and Kerwin waiting for them.

"What shall we do?" Tom asked as he descended back into his body.

Willet replied, "Judging by Oriana's appearance, there's more explaining to do than last time. Let me do the talking."

Tom awoke to see Oriana standing over him with her arms crossed. The expression on her face reminded him of his mother when he was once caught with some "borrowed eggs" from the neighbors coop.

Tom could feel his vocal chords tighten as she bent over him and said, "Have a nice sleep? Or whatever it is that you do?"

Tom felt like a mouse being pounced upon by a cat. He looked nervously at Willet beside him.

Willet growled, "Leave Tom alone! You have frightened the life out of both of us with your sudden appearance in our camp!" He tried to play the part of a grumpy old man rudely awakened from a sound sleep.

"That's precisely what I'm beginning to think!" Oriana replied with a smirk. "This is the second time that I've seen you both go near as stone cold as two corpses only to return to normal in the blink of an eye."

Willet acted mildly annoyed as he complained, "I've told you that Tom and I are magicians and we occasionally meditate together."

"You will have to do better than that this time because I'm not buying it! There's something else going on and I want to know what it is!"

Willet looked at Tom who just raised his hands and shrugged.

"Very well," Willet sighed. "However, you may find the truth even harder to believe."

"Try me!" said Oriana triumphantly as she sensed that she had won this confrontation.

"Astral projection," Willet softly replied.

"What's that?" demanded Oriana as the smug look on her face turned to a scowl as she became suspicious of more trickery.

"We are able to consciously separate our spirits from our bodies."

"Yes! That explains it!" shouted Kerwin excitedly. "I saw two bright lights settle upon their bodies just before they woke up!"

"Impossible!" blurted Oriana as her scowl gave way to a confused look.

"Not so my child!" Willet replied. "Dreams are but a different form of astral projection. The difference is that dreams are a little known and remembered part of our lives whereas what we do is well remembered."

Willet continued by telling Oriana some of her dreams based on the times that he and Tom had taken her spirit with them. While she did not remember some of what Willet told her, he told her enough to eventually convince her.

Heidi suddenly screamed and the blood drained from her face. "It was you!" she shouted as she backed away from them. "Throm called your names! He saw you! You were there the night Throm left me!"

Heidi covered her face with her hands and dropped to her knees as she cried convulsively.

Tears welled up in Tom's eyes as he knelt before his mother and put his arms around her.

"Mother, it is not what you think," Tom whispered as he tried to comfort her. "We meant no harm."

"No harm!" She repeated as she suddenly stopped crying and looked at him. "You caused his death!" she shouted as she pushed him away.

"Do not be too harsh!" Willet said. "Things are not always as they appear."

"What do you mean?" Heidi asked as her curiosity was aroused. "I saw him disappear into the enchanted lake."

"That is true, however, did you see him die?" asked Willet.

"Not exactly," Heidi responded. "His body was never found."

"Then how do you know for sure that he is dead?"

Heidi's jaw dropped and she stared at Willet in shock and confusion. After several minutes, she collected herself and asked, "What do you mean?"

Willet smiled and said, "Throm is alive!"

Heidi's face went white and she passed out. Oriana caught her and laid her gently down. She cradled her head and felt her pulse. When she determined that Heidi had fainted, Oriana said, "How?"

Willet replied, "Enough has been said for now. King Hostyn and all his household have been slain! We must hurry to Lochlemond before chaos and ruin over take the city."

Together they roused the camp and left for Lochlemond during the night. For the next three days, they pressed forward as fast as possible allowing only a few hours of sleep. Some of the soldiers grumbled and more slipped away until they numbered no more than three hundred by the third day.

Ian rode up to where Tom and Willet were riding and complained, "Izora does nothing while we loose many good fighting men. I fear we will need every one of them and more for the fight that looms before us."

He looked at Willet and said, "Can nothing be done to stop them from leaving?"

Willet closed his eyes as if praying or searching for the right words. When he opened his eyes he said, "Such losses are meant for our good."

"How can this be?" asked Ian.

"We are being purified. Look to the men that remain," said Willet as he gestured with his arm to those behind them. "Each of them has endured much hardship and yet they continue steadfast. They have committed all they are to fight a battle whose odds are greatly against us."

Ian turned around and looked at the ranks of foot soldiers behind them. They looked dusty, thirsty and tired. As he stared at them, his eyes locked with one of the men in the front rank and they exchanged a brief smile. In that smile,

Ian saw great courage and dedication. He bowed his head in a sign of respect and the soldier's smile grew. The soldier returned the gesture and Ian realized that what Willet said was true. He felt a strong bond of unity in mind and purpose that drove them to sacrifice all for the cause of *The Past and Future King.*

LOCHLEMOND

HREE DAYS LATER, THEY REACHED the plain before the Dileas River. On the opposite side of the river, the walls of Lochlemond formed a wide arc that spread for miles to their right and left. On their left, Tom could see the two massive towers that marked the entrance of the channel that connected the harbor to river. On their right, the upper part of the city and the palace were visible beyond the cliffs which separated it from the lower part. It was as Tom remembered it except for numerous plumes of black smoke that told him that this visit would be different.

When they reached the river, Willet halted the column and said, "Tell the men to shine their armor and bathe to prepare for the Princess of Lochlemond!"

Ian and Izora readied their men and several hours later they reformed their ranks. Tom and Willet resumed their places at the head of the column. After waiting for several minutes, Tom asked, "Why do we wait?"

Willet pointed to a nearby thicket beside the river and said, "Behold! The Princess of Lochlemond!"

Oriana emerged from the thicket on a white horse and galloped to the head of the column. Everyone was captivated by her appearance. She wore a long white silk dress embroidered with pearls, a multi-color necklace and the diamond crown that Tom had seen her wear in Camlin. She shimmered as the sunlight reflected from the pearls and precious stones that covered her body. However, even more striking was her face and demeanor. She rode with elegance and dignity that Tom had not seen before. She seemed to float towards him in slow motion with so much beauty and grace that she took his breath away.

Oriana smiled and nodded her head to Tom and Willet as she passed by. Tom thought to himself, "She rides with amazing confidence as if she were returning to her home rather than as a stranger going to an uncertain fate."

When she reached the head of the column, Willet shouted, "Long-live the Princess of Lochlemond!"

Tom found himself shouting with the others, "Long-live the Princess of Lochlemond!"

They crossed the Dileas River and advanced towards the main gate. As they approached, Tom's stomach tightened as he saw that the gate was open and there was great confusion. Some were trying to get into the city hoping for refuge from Andhun's advancing armies while others were trying to escape the chaos within. This produced a tangled mass of shouting and pushing people who largely ignored their approach. Tom's hands became clammy and his heart began to pound as a wave of fear engulfed him. He suddenly realized the magnitude of lawlessness and confusion that had settled on this vast city.

"Great Creator protect and help us!" Tom prayed to himself. "We are lost without you!"

Immediately, he felt a surge of energy from the invisible seeing stone around his neck and he shouted, "Hail Princess Oriana!"

"Hail Princess Oriana!" shouted the men behind him in reply.

The trumpeters in their column sounded their horns which drew the attention of the crowd.

What happened next surprised everyone for the crowd turned towards them and stood absolutely still. A white light like a faint halo surrounded Oriana. The crowd backed away from her in amazement and some dropped to their knees. The light gradually intensified until some of the people shielded their eyes as she passed. Soon the crowd joined the soldiers as they repeated the salute, "Hail Princess Oriana!"

Thus did they pass through the crowd and into the city. Their ranks continued to swell as those inside the city ran to see what was happening. Oriana led them with regal dignity and grace waving and smiling as though she was a familiar princess returning from a long absence.

Tom noticed that Oriana did not seem startled or surprised by her glowing personage. He was so absorbed by her beauty that it took him awhile before he noticed that he too was glowing! When he looked around, he saw that everyone in their column was surrounded by the same white light but with less intensity than Oriana.

Kerwin shouted, "Praise the Great Light our Creator who has made us soldiers of light!"

Willet shouted, "Praise the Great Light!" which was repeated by the crowd that surrounded them.

Willet leaned over to Tom and whispered in his ear, "Kerwin and this crowd see the light that has been given to us. However, Oriana and the others in our troop do not see it yet they are blessed by it. Such are the blessings of the Creator. They are not experienced in the same way by all."

Thus was the City of Lochlemond conquered in a day without a single bow shot. Everyone who saw Oriana was awed by her brilliance. In the days to come, the light surrounding her gradually faded but not before she became their queen and order was restored. However, there were some who bowed to their new queen but remained loyal to Andhun.

THE STORM GATHERS

OVER THE NEXT FEW WEEKS, the river of refugees entering Lochlemond slowed to a trickle and then abruptly stopped. Inside the city, the defenders frantically prepared for the arrival of Andhun's armies. Oriana placed Tom and Willet in charge of the defense of the lower city while Ian, Izora and Heidi were responsible for the upper city. For Tom, the days passed in a blur of unrelenting details related to stockpiling and rationing food, settling refugees, organizing the defenses, judging crimes and dealing with complaints.

It was late afternoon on a chilly autumn day when Andhun arrived. Tom and Willet were overseeing the placement of a floating log and chain boom just inside the entrance to the harbor when alarm bells sounded at several places along the wall.

"Look to the sea!" Willet shouted as he went to the edge of the parapet and looked through an eyepiece.

Everyone nearby stopped what they were doing and rushed to the top of the wall. Tom stood beside Willet but he did not see anything unusual until Willet handed him his eyepiece.

The channel that connects the harbor to the Dileas River was about a mile upstream of its confluence with the Capacian Sea. The wall surrounding the old city formed a "U" shaped curve roughly five miles long that was anchored on either end by the cliffs upon which the new part of the city was built. The walls of the old part of the city were within one hundred feet of the shoreline and all but two miles faced the Sea. Hence, there were only two gates one on either side of the "U" shaped wall near the cliffs. The old city was built on marsh land and filled the space between the wall and the harbor. It formed a ring around the harbor that ranged from a hundred feet to one mile wide. Because the harbor occupied most of the interior, the majority of the dwellings were house boats connected by wooden planks that functioned as city streets.

Most of the old city had been evacuated except for soldiers, constables and fire brigades. Their plan was to station most of their men near the gates with a mobile reserve on horses to defend the rest of the wall. Between the gates, a single thin line of soldiers and citizen militia was all that could be mustered.

Tom looked down the Dileas River towards the sea and scanned the horizon. He stared in amazement and awe at the kaleidoscope of multi-shaped sails that grew slowly taller as the fleet approached. The sails were like a dense forest that stretched as far as Tom could see.

"There are more than I expected," Willet said softly as if talking to himself.

"What shall we do?" asked Tom as he handed the eye piece back to Willet.

Before Willet could reply, several loud explosions sounded behind them. Tom turned to see rockets shooting into the sky from the upper city.

Willet said, "It appears that Andhun has also arrived by land. We should not expect any help from our friends up there."

Willet took another look at the approaching fleet and yelled, "Abandon the walls!"

"Why?" asked Tom.

"There is a line of fire galleys ahead of the fleet!"

Tom again looked into the eyepiece. He could now see hundreds of fire galleys leading the invading fleet. Each fire galley was propelled by a hundred oarsmen and had a serpent head through which flaming liquid could be shot for several hundred feet. Each serpent head could be swiveled to increase the range of their destructive fire.

Willet explained, "With their shallow draft, the fire galleys will be able to beach themselves while engulfing the walls in flames.

Tom's heart sunk as he heard this. It seemed like they were defeated before the battle had begun. "Is there nothing we can do?

Willet looked at Tom. He could see the desperation in his eyes. "Do not give up hope. All is not lost. We must choose wisely how and when to fight. To stand our ground on these walls would result in the foolish loss of many good men. There is nothing sacred about these walls so let's let them in and prepare a warm welcome for them."

Willet smiled at Tom and slapped him on the back. Tom's despair melted and he returned the smile as he realized that Willet had a plan.

FIGHTING FIRE WITH FIRE

$\mathcal{W}$HILE ANDHUN'S FLEET APPROACHED THE city, Willet ordered several barges full of boulders to the entrance of the harbor where they were scuttled. These barges had previously been prepared for this purpose. Long metal rods were mounted to the decks which prevented any ships from entering. They had thirty fire galleys which they divided into two groups. Tom commanded one and Willet the other. These ships were sent to the back side of the harbor where they could reach the walls with their fire. The rest of the fighting ships containing catapults and ballistas were arranged in a semi-circle just inside the log boom. The logs were connected by short lengths of chain and both were wrapped in a fire resistant fabric made from the bark of the Toyon tree. From this arrangement, their ships could fire upon virtually all of the walls.

The soldiers and militia were concentrated in two defensive lines on both sides of the harbor. They used streets that ran from the junction of the walls and the cliffs to the harbor. Along these streets, they formed two solid walls by boarding up buildings and barricaded any openings between them. This perimeter was then covered with Toyon fabric and doused with water pumped from ships in the harbor.

Shortly after they completed their new defenses, several sections of the wall facing the Capacian Sea burst into flames. The flames spread as more fire galleys reached the shore until the entire wall was engulfed in flames that spread into the city in various places. After several hours, the flames subsided and the wall reappeared as scorched stone. A smoky haze settled over the city and a tense silence ensued that was interrupted by the crackling of burning wood and the occasional collapse of a burning building.

Tom paced the deck of one of their fire galleys stopping occasionally to scan the vacant city walls. He dreaded the assault that he knew was coming but he also wished it would get started. He wondered what was happening in the upper city and sent a runner to find out. Finally, he mumbled to himself, "What are they waiting for?"

An old sailor nearby spat on the deck and said, "Darkness."

Tom replied, "Send some men in small boats to watch the walls and signal us when they appear."

"Aye Sir!" said the old sailor and gathered some men.

Tom looked at the thick grey clouds and thought to himself, "This will be a dark night with no moonlight to guide us." He felt alone and inadequate to command thousands of men. He wished that Willet was with him.

As if in response, Tom felt a warm sensation on his chest and he realized that he would never again be alone. A familiar voice sounded inside of his head, "Have no fear. I am near."

"Egric!" whispered Tom and he smiled as he felt a surge of confidence and energy.

It was pitch dark when a dozen red rockets announced the presence of the invaders on the walls. In the glow of the rockets, Tom could see the silhouettes of thousands of men climbing over the walls. He looked across the harbor and saw a green rocket arc high over the water. Willet was signaling him to attack.

"Fire!" shouted Tom.

The men nearby ignited the Greek fire. A fountain of flames shot from the head of the dragon on his ship. The blackness of the night was dispelled by yellow light as fourteen other fountains of flames joined the one from his ship. The flames created an inferno that separated the defenders from the invaders between the harbor and the city wall. Meanwhile, the other ships in the harbor fired flaming projectiles of various sorts into the surrounding city. Soon the harbor was surrounded by a ring of fire. Even the water between the city and their fleet was aflame due to leaking barrels of oil that had been left on the docks. However, the flames did not pass the boom that encircled their ships.

By dawn, the fire had raged throughout the city reducing most of it to a smoldering ruin. A cold, north wind drove the smoke from the city but also brought showers of sleet and rain. Although Andhun's men had been beaten back, Tom knew they were far from beaten. He began to wonder what would happen next when hundreds of horns sounded outside the walls. Immediately, a fountain of flaming meteors shot up into the sky along the entire length of the city walls. Tom momentarily stared in awe at the spectacle of so many objects moving in unison. They arced high into the sky overhead converging above their heads before raining down upon them from three sides.

Tom's heart sank as he realized that Andhun's men had moved trebouchets and catpults up to the other side of the city walls during the night. Flaming boulders covered in pitch fell like rain. Many of their ships were burning or sinking before the next volley was launched.

"Abandon ship!" Tom shouted as two boulders pierced the deck of his ship and embedded themselves in the hull. He jumped into the cold water with his men and swam towards the shore at the back of the harbor. Several times he dove beneath patches of burning oil on the surface.

When he reached the shore, Tom looked back at the burning ships and city. Thousands of men were crawling over the walls like ants. He knew that in minutes they would open the gates and a flood of invaders would descend upon them. Already there was a hail of arrows flying back and forth along their defensive lines. Tom's heart sank as he realized that they would not be able to hold their defensive positions.

The lower and upper cities were connected by a tunnel that ran from the base of the cliff to the palace in the center of the upper city. This tunnel was about twenty feet high and wide. It gradually sloped upwards until it emerged in a wide plaza near the palace. A large iron gate that could be raised into the roof of the tunnel by two massive chains and a winch controlled the entrance.

Tom looked towards the opposite side of the harbor and saw that Willet's men were already engaged in hand to hand fighting. It would not be long before his men would also face a flood of invaders as they massed along the defensive line on his side.

"You must retreat and save those you can," said a voice inside Tom's head.

"Egric!" thought Tom as he recognized the voice.

"Sound the retreat!" Tom shouted to a nearby bugler who blew his horn.

Soon the retreat signal resounded on both sides of the harbor. Flaming boulders began to fall along the defensive lines as Andhun's men gradually shifted their fire from the ships to the shore. Tom picked up a sword and shield from a fallen soldier and ran to the perimeter of the fighting. As he ran, his senses sharpened and time seemed to slow down. He felt Egric's presence which gave him confidence and a keen sense of his surroundings. He soon found himself in the midst of the fighting. Although he moved with unnatural quickness and slew scores of foes, he could feel that his men were slowly being forced backwards towards the tunnel entrance.

Willet suddenly appeared beside him and shouted, "The gate! Look to the gate!"

Tom glanced over his shoulder and a wave of fear engulfed him. The gate at the entrance to the tunnel was down!

"Move to the gate!" Willet shouted as he covered Tom's retreat.

A second wave of fear washed over him when he reached the gate and looked inside. A dozen paces inside the gate the winch used to raise the gate was padlocked. They were trapped outside the gate and there was nobody inside to help them!

"Treachery!" Willet shouted as he surmised their

predicament. "This is the work of some of Andhun's cronies in our ranks!"

"What shall we do?" asked Tom.

"You must raise this gate!" Willet replied.

"But that's impossible!" said Tom as he gripped the heavy metal bars of the gate. "It takes four men to turn the winch when it is unlocked."

"Nothing is impossible! I saw how the light from your seeing stone made it possible for us to conquer this city. You must believe and have faith! There is a force a work within you that has manifested itself even in this world."

Willet grabbed Tom by the shoulders and looked deeply into his eyes. "Concentrate! Remember what you did when we entered this city! The way will be shown if you trust and seek for what has already been given to you!"

Fear again welled up within Tom as he realized that their survival depended on him. Willet loosened his grip on Tom and backed away but maintained eye contact. Tom saw confidence and hope in Willet's eyes that strengthened him. Willet bowed to him in the manner of the elves and then returned to the fighting.

Tom realized that Willet honored him and saw something more than Tom felt within himself.

"Lift up the gate. I will help you," said Egric's voice inside his head.

Tom grabbed the bars and lifted. The gate did not budge and Tom thought "It's too massive for me."

Egric replied, "For you it is but not for both of us!"

Tom continued to lift and strained with the effort. He stopped breathing as he concentrated in giving his full effort.

At first he thought that he was hallucinating but the gate started to shift slightly and the chains on the winch tightened. He looked at the padlock on the winch and noticed that it too was moving. A few seconds later there was a loud cracking sound as the lock broke and the gate suddenly moved upwards.

Tom rested the bottom of the gate on his shoulders and breathed again. He thought to himself, "Thanks Egric!"

Tom held the gate as the defenders were slowly forced inside by overwhelming numbers of attackers who continued to converge on the tunnel entrance.

Willet suddenly reappeared near Tom as the leading edge of the attackers approached the gate.

"Lower the gate!" shouted Willet.

Tom did not respond as he did not want to trap Willet and some of their men who were still outside the gate. He didn't know what to do but then he thought, "Egric! Do something!"

"Egric's voice inside Tom's head replied, "I can do no more. It is all I can do to hold the gate up."

"What then shall I do?" thought Tom.

Egric responded, "Pray!"

Tom remembered his prayer when they entered Lochlemond and he repeated it. "Great Creator protect and help us for we are lost without you!"

A burst of energy exploded from Tom's chest and moved outward like a shock wave that temporarily blinded and knocked down the invaders. However, the soldiers of Lochlemond were oblivious to what happened but stood dumbfounded as the attackers fell backwards.

"Everyone inside!" commanded Willet.

The remaining defenders entered the gate and Tom lowered it before the invaders recovered. Tom grabbed a spare padlock and secured the winch.

"Form a shield wall and fall back into the tunnel!"

The attackers soon recovered and shot volleys of spears and arrows through the bars of the gate. Tom and Willet organized their archers behind the shield wall and exchanged volleys until the attackers suddenly withdrew.

"Why did they pull back?" Tom asked.

Willet peered into the smoky haze outside the gate and listened intently.

"They come!" said Willet. "Prepare another volley of arrows on my command!"

Tom listened intently but heard nothing. He was about to question Willet when the low rumble of many kettle drums and the stomping of thousands of feet shook the ground. A massive shadow emerged from the haze and slowly moved towards the gate. A huge metal ram's head appeared and slammed into the gate.

"Iron battering ram!" shouted Willet as the head swung backwards and then slammed into the gate again.

"Fire!" shouted Willet and a shower of arrows flew towards the gate.

The battering ram continued to operate despite their volleys of arrows. Although scores of attackers fell, there were many replacements for those who were hit. A few more swings and the bars of the gate began to buckle.

"Fall back!" Willet ordered. "They will soon be through the gate."

Tom and the others defenders backed into the tunnel and then turned and ran up the incline when they were beyond the range of the arrows. The two massive metal doors at the upper end of the tunnel slowly opened as they approached. Oriana and Kerwin stepped out to meet them. Both were dirty, cut and bruised from the battle for the upper city.

Oriana had a sword and dagger in her hands while Kerwin carried only a stout wooden staff.

Tom thought he saw a brief look of relief on Oriana's face when she glanced at him. Oriana asked, "What happened?"

"The lower city has fallen," Willet replied. "We must prepare a reception for those who will soon follow us."

Oriana pointed to a trap door in the ceiling above them and said, "We are ready."

A WARM RECEPTION

THE TRAP DOOR ABOVE THE tunnel was part of a separate and smaller tunnel that opened under the palace. Tom looked up through the opening in the ceiling and could see soldiers moving about in the room above them. The steady booming sound of the battering ram suddenly stopped.

"They're coming!" said Willet.

"Everyone inside!" ordered Oriana.

Once they were safely inside, the doors were shut and bolted. Tom looked through one of several narrow slits in the doors. It wasn't long before he saw a river of torches approaching. When the invaders reached the gate, the trap door in the ceiling opened and hot oil poured into the tunnel. Tom saw the torch flames explode into a fire ball that moved down the tunnel as the flowing oil ignited. The invaders inside were trapped by the advance of those behind them and most of them perished in the flames and thick smoke. Tom turned away from the intense heat and smoke that began to billow through the door slit.

Oriana said, "They will not enter that way. Come! We have much to discuss and even more to do."

Oriana told them that the attack on the upper city failed but only barely as Andhun's forces managed to get several assault towers up to the wall. Fierce hand to hand fighting ensued but, despite courageous leadership and the concentrated efforts of every man who could bear arms, the attackers advanced. When it looked like they would break through, the citizens of Lochlemond armed themselves with knives, clubs and tools of various sorts and swarmed to the aid of the defenders to beat back the attack.

During the next week, Andhun consolidated and reorganized his forces for another assault. Two lines of trebuchets, ballistas, catapults and rocket tubes were moved into position until they stretched for miles before the city. Over a hundred thousand soldiers marched into their assigned places with pomp and precision.

The seventh day was cold and grey. A steady north wind drove the dark clouds across the sky and a few snow flakes flittered through the air. Izora stood beside Tom on top of one of the two towers beside the main gate. Izora was smoking a wooden pipe carved in the shape of a serpent. He took a long pull on his pipe and said, "I'll wager that they don't fight as well as they parade about."

Tom laughed and said, "I would not trade a hundred of them for one like you."

Izora bowed towards Tom in acknowledgement of the compliment. He then again gazed out on the vast army before them. He seemed deep in thought as he took several more puffs in his pipe before he said, "I have never seen so large an army nor so many assault weapons. I do not fear fighting the men but I do fear what so many weapons will do to these walls once the bombardment begins."

Tom replied, "It's time to make final preparations. Let's make sure we make them pay dearly for challenging this section of the wall."

Throughout the day, Andhun's armies moved into their positions on the plain before the upper city. The standards of five kingdoms were paraded before the walls to inspire the attackers and intimidate the defenders. There had never been so large an army ever assembled in the history of men. Andhun's soldiers stood in ranks at least one hundred men deep for as far as Tom could see. Behind them were two rows of trebuchets, catapults and ballistas separated by an open space of two hundred feet to allow for the passage of supply wagons. By dusk they were ready and the assault began.

A single red rocket was fired to announce the start of the attack. In response, thousands of projectiles of various sorts battered the walls and defenses. In addition, Andhun revealed a new invention consisting of ten foot long tubes on tripods from which rockets were launched. These rockets exploded on contact which terrified the civilians and demoralized the soldiers.

A vast expanse of burning torches stretched as far as Tom could see outlining the seemingly endless infantry formations. The rolling beat of kettle drums spread from one end of Andhun's forces to the other until the air and ground vibrated from the thunderous sounds. Tom watched as the rows of lights began to move methodically towards him.

Andhun observed the advance of his armies from a mobile observation tower with King Vulpes and Lagopus when numerous horns sounded behind them and to their left. A triangle of moving lights appeared from behind a rise in the plain as a mounted army rapidly approached.

King Vulpes listened closely to the horns and smiled. "Those are the horns of King Abban's army. Hah! It is just like that old vulture to show up on our coat tails and claim part of the spoils!"

Despite recognizing the horns, Andhun felt uneasy and asked, "If that is King Abban, where is King Bruddai?"

As if in answer, more horns sounded behind them and to their right and another triangle of lights emerged from the shadows of the forest.

"There's your answer!" exclaimed King Vulpes. "Vultures rarely travel alone."

Andhun's anxiety increased as he watched the triangles quickly grow and draw near. "The manner and speed of their approach are more like hawks than vultures."

Wini led the advance from the left while King Torin of Redwald drove hard into the right flank of Andhun's forces. They divided their army in two and used the horns of their defeated foes as well as darkness to deceive Andhun's men. Thus, they were able to charge between the two rows of assault weapons setting them on fire. They carried slings and threw skins filled with oil onto the assault weapons which they ignited with their torches as they rode past. The swiftness and unexpected nature of their attack caused hesitation and confusion in Andhun's advancing formations. This enabled Wini and King Torin to drive the length of both sides and meet in the center whereupon they turned and surged through the invaders towards the main city gate.

When Tom realized what was happening, he ordered everyone off the walls and opened the main gate. Tom's men formed a triangle and advanced towards their mounted allies. Faced with this surprise attack and the confusion in their rear, Andhun's formations fell apart and they could not make an organized response. As a result, Tom soon saw the advancing horsemen and recognized Wini.

Tom's heart leaped for joy at the sight of his friend! He pressed forward towards Wini with such ferocity that his men had trouble keeping up with him. Tom also sensed an urgency to meet and retreat quickly before Andhun's armies could recover.

"Wini! Over here!" Tom shouted.

Wini's face lit up when he saw Tom. He drove his horse to him and dismounted giving Tom a hug while the battle surged around them.

"Master Tom I can not tell you how happy I am to see you! I thought you were dead!"

"That thought crossed my mind about you as well," replied Tom. "Where have you been?"

Wini pointed to a stout, grey bearded man on a large grey horse fighting nearby.

"Behold King Torin of Redwald!"

Tom parried the attacks of several foes and they fought back to back as Tom said, "It's time to return to Lochlemond!"

King Torin's horsemen advanced into Lochlemond. Tom and Wini were among the last to pass through the main gate as their forces withdrew inside. King Vulpes was furious at the turn of events but Andhun remained silent in thought. Finally, Lagopus went up to Andhun and said, "Master, what shall we do?"

Andhun did not respond immediately but then he seemed

to suddenly return to himself and said, "I believe we have underestimated our foes."

He smiled slyly at Lagopus who returned his smile and asked, "Master has a plan?"

"Yes, I believe I do. We should meet the leaders within the city and reason with them."

This seemed too simple for Lagopus so he said, "What if they don't agree?"

"Then we shall surprise them," replied Andhun with a wicked grin that caused them both to laugh much to the consternation of King Vulpes.

WHEN FOES MEET

$\mathcal{T}$WO WEEKS LATER ARRANGEMENTS WERE made and the two armies faced each other on the plain before the city. Oriana, Tom, Willet and Kerwin rode out to meet four horsemen waiting for them under a banner of truce mid-way between their assembled armies. Snowflakes began to fall which shrouded the four horsemen and reduced the army behind them to a line of dark shadows.

"Unless my eyes deceive me, a woman leads them," said King Vulpes with disdain.

"Not just any woman," replied Andhun. "That's no doubt the Queen of Lochlemond!"

"Who is she?" asked Lagopus.

The snowfall increased so that the Princess and her escorts remained shrouded until they were close.

"Impossible!" growled King Vulpes as he recognized Oriana. "I'll have her as queen or as a slave before this day is through!"

"Steady my friend," cautioned Andhun. "We must be patient."

When the two parties met, they dismounted and approached each other.

"Well! Well! I should have known that you would be involved in obstructing my efforts to establish peace and order," Andhun said to Willet.

He looked towards Tom and said, "I sense that you must be the lad with my seeing stone. It was rather rude of you to depart from my house so abruptly."

Andhun bowed towards Oriana and said, "Oriana, Queen of Lochlemond! You could have been queen of ten kingdoms in my new order but instead you chose to be the temporary ruler of a fallen city."

Willet said, "Enough of your prattle! Why have you called us?"

King Vulpes started to withdraw his sword as he stepped towards Willet and yelled, "Insolent dog! I shall teach you some manners!"

Andhun raised his arm to restrain King Vulpes and said, "Peace! I have called this meeting to cease this senseless strife!" He looked at Oriana and said in a soothing voice, "You have fought well and have shown yourself to be a worthy leader. There is no need for further death and suffering."

"What do you propose?" Oriana asked.

"Swear allegiance to Devlin and submit to my authority and you may retain your title as Queen of Lochlemond."

"Never!" Oriana replied with disgust.

Andhun frowned and his face turned red as he said, "Consider carefully! Your position is hopeless. Even if you win a few battles, you are surrounded and will starve."

Andhun's anger passed like a dark cloud and his face changed and he continued with a patronizing voice and expression. "You will eventually surrender or be conquered. Unless you have far more help coming than the surprise skirmish that King Torin provided."

King Vulpes stepped towards Oriana with his hands behind his back.

"You are indeed a woman of great spirit and beauty! Come and be my queen! Together we shall rule over many kingdoms in the new order!"

Oriana looked at him with disgust and said, "You are a snake and a disgrace to the office of King! I would rather die than marry the likes of you!"

"As you wish!" replied King Vulpes as he pulled a dagger from behind his back and plunged it into Oriana's side before anyone could react.

Tom drew his sword and charged King Vulpes who parried his blow with his dagger while he drew his sword with his other hand. Oriana's face went white with shock but she stepped back and gripped her side. She drew her sword and fought off Andhun's standard bearer who tried to impale her with the spear bearing the truce flag. Lagopus blew his horn before Kerwin knocked him to the ground with his staff. Immediately, horns sounded up and down the lines of Andhun's armies as they rushed to the attack. In response, the armies of Redwald and Lochlemond also charged.

The snowfall intensified so that the opposing armies rushed forward but could not see each other until they met. Snowflakes stung Tom's face and King Vulpes looked like a shadow although he was only a few feet away. As Tom fought King Vulpes he became desperate to help Oriana. He knew that the colliding armies would soon be upon them so he locked arms with King Vulpes. He head butted him and pushed him backwards; then he backed away and disappeared into the blizzard.

"This way!" Tom heard a familiar voice inside his head and knew that Sir Egric was leading him. After running a few steps, he came upon two shadows wrestling on the ground. Tom lunged at the larger form on top and found himself facing Andhun's standard bearer. Tom stabbed him before he could react and crawled back to Oriana. When he found her, he threw himself onto her and felt the ground shake from the impact of the colliding armies.

The battle was intense but brief as the blizzard conditions made it impossible to tell friend from foe. The combatants struck wildly at each other and the battle dissolved into groups of disoriented men who soon desired only to return to safety. Many soldiers from both sides wound up returning with their foes while thinking they were with friends.

Tom felt a stabbing pain in his leg and suffered many bruises and cuts but resolved to shield Oriana from further harm. Once the combatants had dispersed, Tom pushed himself up so he could see Oriana. She was lying face down as if sleeping. Her face was as white as the snow that covered everything except for a pool of blood that stained the snow beneath her. He turned her over and was relieved when she gave a faint moan. Her eyes opened and she softly said, "Tom!"

"Shh!" replied Tom. "Don't worry. I'm here to take care of you."

A faint smile crossed her face and she said, "You already have."

"What do you mean?"

Oriana whispered, "Before I go, I want you to know that you have captured my heart. I've suppressed and denied my feelings for you but my thoughts kept returning to you."

She squeezed his hand as if to emphasize how much she meant what she said. Tears of joy and sorrow welled up in Tom's eyes and he replied, "I've loved you since the first moment I saw you!" He squeezed her hand and said, "Stay with me! I won't let you go!" He tried to stand but an explosion of pain in his left leg almost caused him to pass out. He collapsed beside Oriana and felt his leg. Midway down his shin he touched bone protruding through skin and realized it was broken.

"Come close my love," she whispered. Tom took a cloak off a dead soldier nearby and covered her. She smiled at him and grabbed a handful of snow.

"It's so beautiful, isn't it! So new and pure!"

"Just like our love!" said Tom.

She pulled him towards her and they kissed.

Tom and Oriana rested in each others arms and gazed into each others eyes. Tom felt deep inward joy in the midst of physical pain and the surrounding destruction. He marveled at how he could feel such warmth inside while he was so cold outside. Then he realized that his seeing stone must be glowing. He felt energy flowing from him and into Oriana. Instinctively, he reached for his invisible stone because it felt somehow lighter.

The snow continued to fall heavily and they were soon covered with a foot of snow. Tom wondered if anyone could find them in such a blizzard.

"Dear Creator, please help us," he prayed as he fell into a deep sleep.

"Tom! Tom!" a familiar voice sounded inside his head.

Tom found himself looking down at Oriana and realized that his spirit had left his body.

"Come quick! We must hurry!" said Egric.

"Where are we going?"

"No time to explain. Follow me!" Egric replied.

Egric led Tom to the tunnel gate that opened into the Upper City. The doors were closed but not bolted. There were several dead guards lying beside the doors. Egric and Tom passed through the doors and entered the tunnel. Inside, Andhun's men were hoisting wooden kegs of black powder up through the trap doors in the ceiling.

"What are they doing? Where are the rest of the guards?"

Egric replied, "Traitors in your ranks have dispatched the few guards on duty who were loyal. While Andhun pretended to discuss peace, his men have gained entrance to the city and are placing explosive powder kegs beneath the palace."

"We must warn Willet!" said Tom.

"In due time," counseled Egric. "First I must show you something else."

Egric took Tom inside the palace walls to a large, two-tiered fountain in the courtyard. A sheet of ice over ten feet wide had formed from the overflow of water from the upper basin to the lower one.

Egric said, "Approach the ice sheet."

Tom crossed the snow covered ice in the lower basin and paused before the flow ice. A faint yellow glow appeared deep inside that gradually grew brighter. Tom stood riveted not so much by what he saw as by what he heard. As the light intensified, Tom heard singing but it was unlike anything ever heard in the world of men. Tom closed his eyes and listened intently. He heard sweet chanting in an elfish tongue that ended abruptly.

After a few seconds, the chanting continued but a different voice and direction. Tom's excitement grew as he remembered where he had heard this singing. He opened his eyes and gazed at a landscape that he had not seen for many years.

"The Forest of Glainne!"

"Yes," replied Egric. "Tonight this portal will remain open and those who hear the singing may enter."

Egric continued, "It is time for you to return. Kerwin and Willet are close to your resting place with Oriana."

ESCAPE TO GLAINNE

$\mathcal{W}$ILLET AND KERWIN SEARCHED FOR hours and it was dark when they found Tom and Oriana.

"Master Tom! Wake Up!"

Tom slowly opened his eyes and saw Kerwin's face close to his. Although his eyes stared off into the night, Tom could see the concern on his face and realized that he must feel frozen. Tom smiled briefly with relief at being found but then he became worried and turned towards Oriana.

Willet wrapped Oriana in some blankets and gently lifted her into the back of a wooden cart pulled by a donkey.

"How did you find us in this snowstorm?" Tom asked Kerwin.

Kerwin laughed and said, "The snow slowed us but, once we got close, the green light shining from both of you was a powerful beacon."

Tom put his arm around Kerwin's shoulders and stood up on his good leg. He hopped and got into the cart beside Oriana.

"Dear Kerwin! I'm in your debt."

"On the contrary!" Kerwin replied. "Your kindness and mercy to me when I was a lonely beggar beside the road gave me a new life with devoted friends!"

Willet and Kerwin got into the single seat on the front of the cart and started back to Lochlemond. The snow continued to swirl about them so that they could not see more than a few feet.

"Which way?" asked Willet.

Kerwin turned slowly about in his seat as if trying to sense which way to go.

"That way!" said Kerwin pointing to his right.

"How do you know?" asked Willet.

"I don't!" Kerwin replied. "Listen!"

Willet closed his eyes and focused his attention in the direction Kerwin was pointing. After a few seconds, he smiled and said, "Your hearing is keen indeed! Unless the wind or my imagination deceives me, I believe I hear a song that is not of this world."

Kerwin replied, "I agree. I have never heard such marvelous singing! It thrills me to the bone and I feel drawn to it!"

"So do I," said Willet wistfully. "Let's find it's source."

Despite the snowstorm that blinded them, they followed the singing back to Lochlemond and through its streets. As they drew near to the fountain by the palace, they encountered soldiers and citizens who were also captivated by the enchanted singing. When they reached the fountain, a crowd had gathered. Willet drove the cart slowly through the crowd by shouting, "Make way for the Queen of Lochlemond!"

When they reached the fountain, Willet drove the cart over the low wall of the lower basin. They crossed the snow covered ice until they reached the portal in the flow ice where Willet stopped the cart.

Kerwin asked "Why are we stopping? Is something wrong?"

Kerwin's questions shook Willet out of his enjoyment of the landscape before them. A dirt path a few feet away invited them into a forest of giant trees. In the distance, there was a lush green valley with water falls.

Willet replied, "No, everything is fine." He turned to the crowd behind them and said, "Citizens of Lochlemond and Redwald! Before us is a path to a new life! Do not be afraid! Behold!"

Willet drove the cart straight into the flow ice and entered the path in the forest. He got off of the cart and walked back through the flow ice and faced the crowd.

"As you can see, the ice is not a barrier but a window to a better place. Come and join your queen!"

Wini emerged from the crowd and boldly walked through the flow ice. He walked over to the cart and turned back towards the crowd.

"Don't be afraid! Come!" Wini beckoned to the crowd.

This demonstration plus the attractive scene and enchanting music moved a few of the bystanders to pass through the portal. Once the crowd saw them safely standing beside the cart, they surged forward and also entered the portal. Willet rejoined Kerwin and drove the cart down the path towards the Valley of Glainne. Wini walked beside the cart as thousands of men, women and children followed.

The warm air and sweet fragrance of flowers mingled

with the singing that came from invisible sources in the surrounding forest.

Oriana stirred and Tom bent over her and kissed her on the lips. She opened her eyes and smiled.

"Tom! My love!" she said. "Are we alive?"

She looked up and around at the surrounding forest. She saw Wini and the crowd behind them and asked, "Are we the souls of those who have died. Are we going to paradise?"

Wini laughed and said, "No, my lady! We are very much alive. We are going to a place as close to paradise as there is on this side of death."

"Where would that be?" she asked.

"The Valley of Glainne!" Willet replied. He turned the cart around. Before them the path descended into a lush, green valley. She saw several waterfalls on the far wall of the valley that flowed into a large lake in its center.

"Never have I seen such a beautiful and peaceful place!" Oriana exclaimed with wonder.

"Behold the Valley of Glainne!" exclaimed Willet with great joy.

REUNION

*T*OM LOOKED ACROSS THE VALLEY and his thoughts took him back in time to when he had last visited this place as a youth. As he recalled the familiar details, his eyes paused when he looked at the large lake in the center of the valley. He was surprised to see that where there was once a single cottage there was now a city that glowed from thousands of lights.

Oriana partially removed the blankets covering her and gasped with surprise. A bright green light temporarily blinded her when she looked at the seeing stone around her neck. She replaced the blankets and, after recovering her sight, she slowly brought it out again. This time the stone did not shine with as much intensity. When Tom saw this, he reached for his seeing stone and took it out from under his shirt. It too was glowing with a brilliant, green light.

"How can this be?" he thought to himself.

Egric's voice inside his head replied, "Feel the chain!"

When Tom felt the chain around his neck, he understood what had happened. Instead of the double chains resulting from the fusion of the two stones at the tomb of Sir Egric, there was now only one.

"You have carried my seeing stone to its rightful owner," said Egric.

Wini laughed as he looked at the puzzled faces of Tom and Oriana. He reached inside his shirt and pulled out his glowing stone. He abruptly stopped laughing when something caught his eye.

"Look!" Wini shouted excitedly as he pointed down the path. "There's another green light!"

Everyone inside the cart looked down the path. At first Tom saw nothing but the multitude of yellow lights from the dwellings by the lake. Then he saw it. A single faint green light left the city lights and was rapidly approaching them up the path. As it got closer, it grew brighter and began to bob up and down. When it was almost upon them, Tom saw a large shadow moving rapidly towards them. The darkness prevented Tom from recognizing Min until he was upon them.

"Min!" shouted Wini as he ran towards the giant shadow. The two collided and Min picked Wini up and swung him around like a rag doll.

"Wini! Dearest of friends!" laughed Min.

The crowd behind them grew frightened at the sight of the troll and several soldiers drew their weapons.

"Don't be afraid!" Willet shouted to the crowd. "This creature will not harm you!"

Willet jumped from the cart and gave Min a hug. The crowd relaxed somewhat but remained guarded until they saw how affectionate Min was. He gently hugged Tom, Oriana and Kerwin while laughing and prancing about with such joy that the crowd became at ease with the strange creature.

"This is a most blessed day! My heart leaps for joy at the sight of each of you!" Min said. "However, lest I be selfish, I must take you to others who anxiously wait to greet you!"

Min led them down the path to the dwellings below. When they reached the first cottage, Willet stopped the cart. Tom turned and looked forward. He saw a hooded figure standing in the road.

"Wes Ou Hail!" Welcome!" shouted a familiar voice.

"Prince Caelin!" shouted Tom. "I'm here!"

Prince Caelin bowed to Willet and Kerwin and walked to the side of the cart. He removed his hooded cloak revealing gleaming armor. He bowed to Tom and Oriana and said, "Welcome to Glainne! Heroes of Lochlemond and Redwald!"

Tom looked down and said, "You do us too much honor for we are the fleeing remnants of a defeated army. Look and you will see cold, tired and wounded soldiers and civilians."

"Nay! Master Tom! I see the faithful and chosen servants of the Creator who have entered our world in numbers never before thought possible! It is surely a sign of the dawning of a new age!"

Prince Caelin smiled and continued, "This time we shall have a proper celebration of your arrival!" He motioned towards the city where suddenly thousands of elves carrying torches appeared and lined the street before them. The elves sang a sweet song that Tom recognized as the same one that the elves of Taliesin sang when he entered their city many years ago. The elves bowed as they passed and their faces were so full of joy that Tom felt like they were long separated family members finally reunited. Thus, did the ragged refugees of Lochlemond enter The Vallley of Glainne as heros.

TEST OF FAITH

$\mathcal{T}$HE LINE OF PEOPLE ENTERING the portal gradually diminished to a trickle and then to a few stragglers. Heidi stood beside the portal and argued with herself.

"This must be an illusion. Yes, it's a bad dream." She told herself. "This cannot be real." She wrung her hands and paced nervously back and forth. She had watched Tom, Oriana, Willet and even King Torin pass before her eyes through the flow ice.

"I must wake up!" she said to herself as she pinched herself and said, "Wake up!"

Part of her wanted to return to the warmth of her bed but the enchanted singing and beauty of the forest scene before her beckoned to her.

As she wrestled with herself, she heard a voice softly call her name.

"Heidi! Heidi!"

She tensed so much that she stopped breathing and her

heart pounded in her head. She stared intently into the flow ice to see the source of the voice.

"No! It can't be!" she shouted to herself as she both denied and grew excited by the voice.

"Throm?" she whispered.

Two hooded figures stepped out of the woods and onto the path. Their faces were hidden as they walked towards her. When they were a few paces away, one of them pulled back his hood. Heidi stared in amazement at what looked like a young man with pointed ears dressed in gleaming armor.

"Greetings Heidi!"

"Who are you?" she asked.

"I am Cearl," son of Prince Caelin.

"He is an elf," said the other hooded figure.

"Throm?" Heidi asked again as she shivered.

"Yes, my love! It's me!" Throm said as he pulled back his hood to reveal his face.

Heidi stood speechless for several minutes and then said, "You are dead! Now I know I must be dreaming!" She started to back away from the portal.

"Please! Don't go!" pleaded Throm. "I am very much alive."

"I don't believe you!" Heidi shouted. "This is just a bad dream!"

Throm grew concerned but gently replied, "If you leave me, I will remain but a memory to you. However, if you come to me, we will be together forever!"

Tears streamed down Heidi's face and she began to tremble.

"I can't! I have to keep my feet on the ground! You are just an illusion!"

She continued, "If you are real, then come to me!"

Throm stepped to the portal and tried to pass through it. He bumped into an invisible barrier just as he reached her. He took a step back and said, "I can't pass to you. There is a will greater than mine that controls this passage."

Throm placed his hand against the invisible barrier and looked deeply into Heidi's eyes. "I love you! Trust me, my love! Place your hand here and see if I am a ghost!"

Heidi slowly raised a shaky hand while she stared into Throm's eyes. A tingling sensation spread from her finger tips to her toes as their hands met and she felt his warm flesh.

"Throm! My love! I'm yours!" she shouted as she stepped through the portal and embraced him. They held each other tightly for several minutes. Heidi drank deeply into her senses the touch, smell and sight of her husband.

"I don't know how this can be but I pray that it never ends."

Throm kissed her and said, "I assure you that you have just taken a step of faith into a bigger and better life!"

EPILOGUE

$\mathcal{I}$T WAS MIDNIGHT WHEN A loud explosion rocked the city of Lochlemond and sent shock waves through the earth. The blast lifted the palace into the air and then it came crashing down in total ruin. Thousands of Andhun's soldiers poured out of the tunnel gate and quickly subdued any resistance.

Andhun sat beside a fireplace with Lagopus inside his command post. He smiled when he heard the explosion and said, "Thus ends the Kingdom of Lochlemond."

"And the last of the resistance to your new order!" Lagopus added.

They both smiled and sat in silence until Lagopus asked, "Will you bring the others into this world now that the new order has begun?"

Andhun stirred uneasily since he still had not figured out how he managed to bring Lagopus into the human world. He tried to appear calm and aloof as he replied, "In due time! There are still a few bands of rebels to dispose of."

"Who are they?" Lagopus asked.

Andhun replied, "Their leader goes by the name of Cyric of Camlin."

A powerful earthquake shook Hadrian's Keep at the same moment that the Palace of Lochlemond was destroyed. There was a burst of white light in the library at Hadrian's Keep that blinded Cebu and the other dwarves who were near the great white rock. They were thrown onto their faces and remained motionless for several minutes. Cebu blinked and rubbed his eyes as his sight gradually returned. He looked up at the massive white rock. The symbols on the rock were altered and two thirds of them became legible. Cebu began to read aloud:

> *I will destroy the wisdom of the wise.*
> *The intelligence of the intelligent I will*
> *frustrate.*
> *For my ways are not your ways,*
> *Nor are my thoughts your thoughts.*
>
> *Great and marvelous are my plans!*
> *For as far as the heavens are above the earth,*
> *So are my thoughts beyond your*
> *understanding.*
>
> *Now comes a new dawn.*
> *When what is not shall be.*
> *Weeping may endure for a night,*
> *But joy comes in the morning!*

Therefore, look to what has been
And trust in what can be.
For the weak shall become strong,
Sons of might!
Sons of light!

Although the dwarves diligently studied these words, they could not agree on their meaning. Cebu remembered his grandfather's words to interpret prophesies using only *The Once & Forever Ruler*.

Despite the many years he had lived with the dwarves, he remained loyal to the teachings of his grandfather. He managed to find a copy of this outlawed book in a dusty pile on the lower level of the library. He used this forbidden book to interpret the words on the sacred rock. He smiled to himself at the foolishness of the other dwarves to seek truth without using *The Once & Forever Ruler*.

Cebu concluded that the words spoke of Devlin's higher wisdom and ways. He looked forward to the time when his brethren, the gnomes, would return to rule the Forbidden Mountains. Although he was troubled by the meaning of the reference to the sons of men and light, he figured the meaning of these last words would become obvious when the remaining words were known. He was certain that the time had come for him to fulfill his destiny. He would find a way to contact his brethren and open to them a hidden passage into the Forbidden Mountains!

Book Review Request

THANK YOU FOR TAKING YOUR valuable time to read my book.

I hope you enjoyed reading it as much as I enjoyed writing it. What did you think? I want to know. I would appreciate if you would take a few minutes to write a review for this book on Amazon.com. Thank you in advance for taking the time to respond. I look forwardto reading your review.

Characters

Abban—King who invades the kingdom of Redwald to force it to submit to the Brotherhood of Andhun.

Aigneis—Angels who remained obedient to God. The elves and fairies are the physical descendants of these good angels on earth.

Alric—King of Strathyre and Oriana's uncle who is one of three kings opposed to the Brotherhood of Andhun.

Amhas—Renegade troll who leads a group of bandit trolls.

Andhun—Wizard formerly of the Order Of Alastrine and once had the seeing stone carried by Tom. Founder and head of the brotherhood based on *The Once And Forever Ruler*.

Behlin—Dwarf scribe who became Willet's friend and leader of those who study the sacred runes of Hadrian's Keep.

Belloc—A large demon who is assigned by Devlin to lead the search for a seeing stone.

Berin—Ancient king of the dwarves and ancestor of King Raegenheri.

Bill Barley—Peddler who delivered books to Willet in Downs End.

Boroc—Orc possessed by a demon. He leads a band of orcs in search of Min.

Bournemouth—Trusted advisor of King Alric of Strathyre who secretly was a member of the Botherhood of Andhun.

Bruddai—King who invades the kingdom of Redwald to force it to submit to the Brotherhood of Andhun.

Caelin—Elf prince and ruler of the Valley of Glainne.

Cath—Strong and young female troll.

Cearl—Elf and son of Prince Caelin assigned to protect Tom.

Cebu—Grandson of Miran who is taken into the Forbidden Mountains upon the death of his grandfather. He seeks to betray the dwarves by revealing an entrance to the Forbidden Mountains.

Ceowulf—Elf of high rank and reputation who strictly follows the traditions and beliefs of his people.

Chadwick—Govenor of a province in the Kingdom of Meglondon. He was killed for his refusal to follow *The Once And Forever Ruler*

Crodha—Orc general who led the attack on the darach trees and obtained Lord Swefred's seeing stone.

Cragmar—Troll searching for an entrance to the Forbidden Mountains.

Cyric—Leader of Camlin which is a village of thieves and bandits. He is the illegitimate son of King Vulpes.

Dehlin—Dwarf son of Behlin and leader of those who guard Hadrian's Keep.

Demonians—Evil angels who followed Devlin in rebellion against their Creator.

Devlin—Demon leader who desires to rule the earth and author of *The Once And Forever Ruler.*

Dinwald—Elf lord who commanded the forces opposed to Devlin in the Battle of Mordula Forest.

Eachan—Young female troll who is talented in sewing and cooking.

Edric—Elf who follows Lord Ceowulf to the Forbidden

Mountains and secretly watches the events surrounding the death of Miran.

Egric—Elf lord who died fighting against Devlin's forces at the Battle of Mordula Forest.

Eni—Elf companion of Cearl who helps Tom escape from werewolves.

Etain—Fairy who serves as scout and messenger for the elves.

Filane—Elf lord who lived with the dwarves in the Forbidden Mountains following the battle of the forest of Modula.

Garash—Head of a band of orc pirates who follow Miran to Hadrian's Keep searching for an entrance to the Forbidden Mountains.

Glyn—Young and attractive female troll.

Gorbash—Demon of Pyrrigian rank charged with guarding Throm and was influential in the conversion of the dwarf Miran to the ways of *The Once And Forever Ruler*.

Hadrian—Dwarf king who built a hidden fortress in the side of Forbidden Mountains named Hadrian's Keep.

Haggert—Demon possessed elder of the Village of Camlin.

Heidi—Mother of Tom.

Hockley—Constable of the Village of Kilkenny who leads villagers in the persecution of those loyal to *The Past And Future King*.

Hostyn—King assassinated in his palace in Lochlemond by traitors loyal to Andhun.

Ian—Lieutenant of Cyric of Camlin assigned to lead Oriana and Tom to Lochlemond.

Izora—Captain of the men-at-arms in the service of King Alric of Strathyre.

Kerwin—Blind man found by Tom on the road to Strathyre.

Kork—Drunken troll at the Black Horse Inn.

Lagopus—Gnome who idolizes Andhun and serves him as his personal attendant.

Linette—Elf princess who raised Willet and rules Taliesin

Olaf—name given to Oriana by Willet as part of her disguise as a boy.

Min—Misfit troll who longs to find friendship.

Miran—Leader and founder of the gnomes. He was once was a dwarf scribe that converted to *The Once And Forever Ruler* which resulted in his banishment from the Forbidden Mountains.

Molech—Chief demon second in command to Devlin and he is in charge of evil spirits roaming the earths.

Nabloth—Young female troll whose mother is Sharat.

Og--Elder female troll from village lead by Sharat.

Olric—Son of King Thymallis and a member of the Brotherhood of Andhun.

Oriana—Princess of Eisendrath and daughter of King Thymallis.

Osric—Elf companion of Cearl who helps Tom escape from werewolves.

Peig—Elder female troll from the village lead by Sharat.

Penda—Elf assigned to protect Wini.

Pyrigians—Elite demons known for their cruelty.

Raegenheri—King of the dwarves.

Ragbar—Demon of Pyrigian rank who was assigned to watch over Andhun.

Ronan—One of the seven kings who support the Brotherhood of Andhun. Led his army against King Alric.

Sharat—Female troll shamman and mother of Nabloth.

Shylah—Troll converted to the ways of The Past & Future King by Min.

Skreel—Eagle and friend of Tom.

Swefred—Elf lord renown as a warrior and keeper of a seeing stone.

Throm—Father of Tom and farmer in the Village of Downs End.

Thymallis—King of Eisendrath and father of Oriana and Olric.

Titans—creatures such as orcs, vampires & trolls formed by the union of evil angels who took human form and intermarried with mankind.

Tom—Son of Throm the farmer and bearer of a seeing stone.

Tondbert—Dwarf who was transformed into a tree by magic.

Torin—King of Redwald who opposes the Brotherhood of Andhun.

Trossacks—Friend of Ian who is the leader of a band of wandering musicians.

Ultan—Troll leader who lead a band of trolls in search of an entrance to the Forbidden Mountains.

Vulpes—King of Meglondon and leader of the kings who support Andhun. Father of Cyric and suitor of Oriana.

Whon—One of the seven kings who support the Brotherhood of Andhun. Led his army against King Alric.

Willet—Scribe of the Village of Downs End, wizard of the Order of Alastrine and mentor to Tom.

Wini—Shepherd of Redwald and companion of Tom.

Witch Of Ogherune—Spirit of a powerful witch who can conjure images of past events.

ABOUT THE AUTHOR

$\mathcal{T}$HE ORIGINS OF MY INTEREST in fiction are rooted in my early childhood. As a child, I loved to sleep over at my friend's house on Friday nights and watch the late night science fiction movies. I have fond memories of ducking in and out of my sleeping bag on the living room floor while being both captivated and frightened.

In college, I discovered the C.S. Lewis and soon was experiencing other worlds in his Space Trilogy and *Chronicles of Narnia*. These were my favorite multi-book stories until a friend suggested I try reading *The Hobbit* by J.R.R. Tolkien. This led to *The Lord of the Rings* Trilogy which I read several times prior to the movies. Hobbits, elves, orcs, trolls were like the races and cultures of man in that they were related but different. Interwoven throughout these stories were the struggle of good and evil as well as the discovery of purpose and realizing one's potential.

My education and career over the past forty years have been in the Environmental Sciences which are hardly conducive to fantasy writing. I graduated with two MS degrees from the University of Wisconsin and worked as a consultant and then as an environmental specialist for a mid-western utility company. After raising two children, I found myself a grandparent with a successful wife who spent several days a week traveling as a director for a dental corporation. My wife claims that being a grandpa has awakened the right side of my brain and has helped me discover my second childhood. I find there is some truth to this as I can act goofy, spoil my grandchildren and then give them back to their parents.

While driving alone on a work trip, a thought occurred to me that I should write a book about what the Bible says about various subjects. I have read the Bible daily for over thirty years, spoken in many churches as a member of the Gideons, taught Sunday School and served as a deacon, so I felt I could help others to understand what I consider the most important book ever written. Two years later my first book, *Truth Seeker: Bible Topics*, was written.

For me writing is a passion. Over the past thirteen years, I have written eight books and over twenty articles for the New York Times about Christianity and Christian Pulse web sites. The *Dawn Herald Triology* is a Lord of the Rings style tale that weaves Christian themes into a multi-book series on the inter-play between reality and fantasy worlds. The spiritual realm, like fantasy, is not real to some but intrigues many people because there is a deep innate sense in mankind that there is a greater reality.

Fictional writing is based on developing interesting characters and then visualizing how they progress in their roles. In other words, the characters carry the plot and writing is like watching scenes in a play unfold. My non-fictional writing revolves around the Bible which I have studied daily for over thirty years. I love to learn and share the awesome truths of the Bible. I am amazed and humbled by what I have written as I see myself as a scribe recording what God has given for our edification.

My *Truth Seeker Series* are five non-fictional books based on the Bible. *Truth Seeker: Bible Topics* summarizes what the Bible says about a wide range of topics with lots of Bible references. *Truth Seeker: Mormon Scriptures & The Bible* summarizes the books upon which Mormonism is based and compares them to the Bible. *Truth Seeker: New Testament Apocrypha* summarizes selected books from the early centuries of Christianity and seeks objective reasons why these books were not included in the Bible. *Truth Seeker: Objections To Christianity* and *Truth Seeker: More Objections To Christianity* are a dialogue with my father who was a critic of Christianity. He summarized his beliefs and problems with the Bible and left me with a written legacy. Thus, these books complete decades of debates that we had prior to his death.

Printed in the United States
By Bookmasters